Fairy Tales For
Little Imps

Edited by Annabel Cook

N e *W*
F i c █ l ● n

New Fiction

First published in Great Britain in 2009 by:
New Fiction
Remus House
Coltsfoot Drive
Peterborough
PE2 9JX
Telephone: 01733 898101
Website: www.forwardpress.co.uk

SBISBN 978-1 85929 161 0

Foreword

When 'New Fiction' ceased publishing there was much wailing and gnashing of teeth, the showcase for the short story had offered an opportunity for practitioners of the craft to demonstrate their talent.

Phoenix-like from the ashes, 'New Fiction' has risen with the sole purpose of bringing forth new and exciting short stories from new and exciting writers.

The art of the short story writer has been practised from ancient days, with many gifted writers producing small, but hauntingly memorable stories that linger in the imagination.

I believe this selection of stories will leave echoes in your mind for many days. Read on and enjoy the pleasure of that most perfect form of literature, the short story.

Parvus Est Bellus.

Contents

The Stories

A Serengeti Story

Jade Azim

It all started when I was separated from my mum. I was only a young cub. Life before was fantastic; I had loads of milk and watched my mum hunt. She was great, and she would risk everything for me. Eventually, of course, this led to the scariest adventure of my life. You see, being a cheetah is a risky business, especially when you live right by a pride of lions. We found this out too late ...

A big male lion looked right into my eyes. I was only a couple of weeks old and never knew the danger that was just before me.

He began stalking and that's when my mum noticed. She ran at top speed to where I was playing and stood between my fate and me. He ran towards her and she stood there. She then looked at me as if to say goodbye. She knew what was going to happen and sneaked in a whisper, 'Run!' But I refused. I wasn't going to leave without her after all she had done for me, but in the end I had no choice. She bared her teeth at the lion and he replied by doing the same. His teeth were twice as big as hers and she knew this. He grabbed hold of her in his mouth and shook her violently. The big male dropped her cold body on the floor without any emotion in his eyes and looked straight at me, licking his lips. I looked at my mum lying lifeless on the floor. 'Bye Mummy,' I whispered tearfully, before running as fast as I could. The lion ran too, but I had a big advantage: cheetahs are the fastest animals on Earth and even at a couple of weeks old I could run at over 40 miles per hour. Eventually I outran him and he never bothered to go any further to catch me. To him, I was just a bite-sized snack!

For ages I ran, crying at the same time. What was I going to do? I grew more and more tired and finally stopped by a large acacia tree; it was the only shade available for miles around. I started to wonder whether I was going to survive or end my life as my mum had ended hers. I was exhausted and decided to rest, despite the unknown dangers around me lurking amongst the grass. I hesitantly closed my eyes before drifting into a deep sleep.

I had a dream, a lovely dream, where I frolicked and played in the shrubs, and with me played my mother. So gracefully did she run and jump, leap and dance without a worry in the world. A herd of prancing gazelles raced across the plains, as did my mum, who fixed an eye on one of the males. With a quick swipe of her paw, the antelope was humanely killed with very little pain. My mum and I sat comfortably in the grass under our favourite tree, eating happily ... Then I woke up and came to my senses. I longed for food and as I was small and the world was huge, there was no way I could possibly feast again.

A family of meerkats suddenly raised their heads over the tall grass. They looked at me and froze, and then they carried on as normal, snatching tiny bugs from the soil. How they could find bugs tasty I don't know, but at the minute, I thought the meerkats were looking very *yummy* indeed. Suddenly, I found myself crouching as low as I could. I placed my paw carefully in front of me, then the other one, until I was just five metres away from them. They turned towards me, twitched and then scurried away. I failed, and I was starving. At this rate I would be dead in a matter of days, but I didn't want to die. I looked out at the horizon and watched the sun disappear. I suddenly realised that it was turning dark and if I was going to survive the night I would have to find a place to hide ... but where?

The Serengeti is a bad place to be after dark, leopards lurk in the shadows, hyenas howl to the moon and lions stalk their next victim. No wonder we cheetahs hide in the night, crouch down in the most secret corner, and shrivel up.

But I was in the middle of it; in the centre of the harshest environment, and the most dangerous of creatures surrounded me. And yet I wasn't so afraid. I thought of my mum, the way she would cuddle up to me when I was scared. She made me feel so secure, so happy.

But reality soon came back to me. I could hear the distant roars of gigantic male lions, and even closer still, the howling of the hyenas. I then heard footsteps and my heart missed a beat. Closer and closer they came until I heard the truth. Something about them seemed familiar; they were not the deafening steps of a lion, but far lighter, more gentle. I stood there for a minute not knowing what would come my way, and then out of the bushes pounced a massive male cheetah. I couldn't believe it. He just stood there glaring into my eyes. 'Could you help me?' I asked in a small voice. 'I really need your help!' He still just stood there but then I realised I had been worrying helplessly about the other predators, when my own kind would look at me as lunch too. He hissed. I yelped. He charged, so I ran as fast as I could. I soared across the open plains and yet he was right on my tail.

'Think fast, think fast,' I kept telling myself, and then I saw it. Out of nowhere, a big boulder stood in my path. It had many holes and cracks in it, but of course I couldn't fit in one of them. Then I saw it, a gap, just wide enough to fit me in it, I lay underneath. So just out of hope, I squeezed into the tiny space I had. The male came to a standstill and skidded right up to the boulder. He looked under with curious yet evil eyes and stared at me. 'I will get you, and I will *kill* you!' he screamed and he disappeared out of sight. I looked back and forth while remaining in all the space I could possibly reach. Then in a flash, his massive paw came swiping inches away from my body. If he tried to get it nearer he would have got stuck, so grumbling at the bottom of his violent voice he walked away.

After a while of waiting in anxiety, I decided to venture out. Nothing was there. It seemed quiet, too quiet! No matter, I crawled on my belly, trying to keep out of sight of any hungry predators. I kept on looking behind, to the right, back behind and then to my left. I continued this for a while until I stopped. I heard a snap, most probably a twig, but a twig only snaps if something makes it, so I froze in my tracks. My breathing got heavy, I tried to tell myself it would be OK, but something in me was saying whatever it was out there wasn't friendly! I followed my instincts and turned back to the boulder, only to notice a hare stood in front of me, unaware of my presence. I was starving and this was my chance to get a well-deserved meal, so I crouched down and thought of how my mum used to do it.

I followed her way, looked where I stepped, kept low. Accelerate, chase, trip and bite … To my amazement, I had caught the hare. It struggled in my mouth until it suddenly stopped. I had done it, my very first kill. I looked down at the dead animal. 'Sorry!' I said sympathetically, and I dragged it under the boulder and squeezed my little body in with it, just in case that male cheetah or some other predator would come to steal it.

Luckily, that night I ate the whole thing with no uninvited guests, and to my delight, had a well-deserved sleep. I did it! I survived my first night as an orphan!

I woke up that morning and reality soon struck. I started crying and shrieked for the comfort of my mum. The Serengeti looked awfully deserted and barren. In my desperation I called and called. 'Help!' I yelled. 'Is anybody out there?'

I got a reply, but I knew it wasn't friendly. It was a faint giggle in the distance, then another, and finally a whole crowd of yelps and giggles echoed not far from me. It came nearer, louder, as if it was mocking me. The giggles were coming from a large group of hyenas and hyenas mean bad news.

I crept towards the boulder I'd slept under, but even though I was going to grow up to be the fastest animal on Earth, I never reached the safety of the boulder in time.

The hyenas crowded around me, showing off their teeth in a wave of sinister smiles, and they giggled and laughed at me. One of the hyenas was blocking the boulder so there was no way to escape. I closed my eyes, ready for my fate. I remembered my mum and the times we spent together, and I took comfort in the thought she would be waiting for me.

I waited for my death, but it seemed far too long. I heard a familiar growl and I opened my eyes. A beautiful cheetah bravely pounced on the group of hyenas, hissing and shrieking at them. The hyenas tried to fight back but the cheetah was surprisingly strong and willing to risk everything. With a bite to the back of the neck, the leader of the hyenas retreated, as did the rest of the clan. They ran over the hills and when they stopped, the cheetah slapped paws on the ground and hissed in great aggression.

I looked at the mysterious stranger that had saved my life and the stranger looked at me. The face, the face was one I had always known. The stranger with formidable strength stood tall. The stranger was my mum! She had survived! I licked and licked her, playing with her in great joy, and she purred in contentment. I laughed in pure happiness. The time I had spent away from her seemed like a lifetime. She had obviously had just as bad a time as me, and I saw on her neck the scars and wounds she bore from the lion that separated us.

She explained to me that to keep her life and mine, she had posed dead on the floor, and when the lion had vanished, she searched for me day and night.

My mum was the cleverest of all cheetahs on the Serengeti, she stood proud in the tall grass and I felt happy again. That night, my mum and I cuddled up tight, just in case anything would dare try to separate us again.

We made the most of our time together until the time came, two years later, when I left to make my own family. As I speak of my life now, I have four cubs and a very beautiful mate, and as I grow old now I share the same story with my loved ones and we live in harmony, knowing my mum is watching over me.

The Lonely Peach

Daniel Eisan

Once upon a time, in a field not so far away, there was a peach tree. It was a beautiful tree. It stood on its own, surrounded by daisies and dandelions and had a view that went on for miles.

Then one day a man called Farmer Green walked up to the tree and said, 'My, my, I'm going to sell a lot of peaches this year.' He started to pick the peaches off one by one and put them into his little basket. Then when his basket was full to the top, he walked back to his van and drove off back to his farm.

Farmer Green unloaded his basket, put the peaches in a bowl and washed them in the sink. He then walked out of the room. All of a sudden the peaches came to life. One by one, out popped a left arm, a right arm, a left leg and a right leg, two eyes, a nose and a mouth. They all looked the same but one was a little different. This peach, Percy, had a keen sense for adventure. He knew he was going to be sold on the market, so instead of staying with the other peaches he jumped off the counter, onto the floor and hid behind the table leg.

Farmer Green entered the room again and started to count the peaches. He thought he had all 49, but as he turned around he saw a peach on the floor. That peach was Percy. Farmer Green walked over, knelt over and picked up Percy. He washed him again and placed him with the other peaches. Percy had a very angry look on his face, but he bottled it up and went to sleep.

Next morning, Percy was woken by the screaming noise of a cockerel. He looked around, rubbed his eyes and said to himself, 'This is the day I will escape.'

Farmer Green walked into the kitchen and said, 'Morning, my little peaches. Today you are going to make me quite a bit of money.' He picked up the peaches and put them into a brown paper bag. Percy managed to hide behind the kettle, barely slipping away from the firm grasp of Farmer Green's rather filthy hand.

Percy stayed hidden until he heard the loud bang of the old wooden door closing behind Farmer Green's back. Percy slowly but surely peeped his head around the side of the kettle, looked around and sighed with relief.

Percy jumped off the counter and headed towards a crack in the door. He just managed to squeeze through. Percy looked around, took a deep breath and began his journey of travelling. 'Here I go,' Percy said to himself. He began to take his first few steps to freedom, being so full of excitement.

Unfortunately Percy was not paying attention to oncoming traffic. He suddenly heard the honk of a speeding lorry. Percy's face dropped, his eyes widened and his mouth gaped. He jumped across to the other side of the road, just missing the wheels. The lorry continued down the road as Percy sat on the grass trying to catch his breath.

Percy got back up, wiped himself down and continued walking. About fifteen minutes later he approached a little village. He walked along the narrow cobbled streets until he saw a little fruit shop. He could smell the strawberries and apples. He slowly approached it. Then suddenly he saw Farmer Green handing a bag of fruit over to an old lady. Percy quickly hid behind a box of grapes. He peeped his head round the corner. He saw that Farmer Green had gone back inside the shop. Percy wiped his brow and said, 'Phew, that was close. I can't imagine what would have happened if I was caught by Farmer Green. I could have been sold off to that lady.'

Percy continued along the cobbled street. He looked up towards the sky. As he did this, the wind started to pick up. Clouds turned grey and started to gather together. Then in one almighty boom, there was a crack of thunder.

Percy had never seen anything like this before. He started to panic. He ran away to find shelter. The rain started to fall all around him. Big splashes of water fell on Percy's head. He fell into a big muddy puddle. He got up, didn't bother to wipe himself down, he just kept on going. Percy quickly turned to go round a corner but a big brown dog started to bark at him and tried to climb a fence to get to Percy.

Percy screamed, quickly turned around and ran towards a place for shelter. Five minutes later he came to an old abandoned shed in the middle of a field. Percy walked inside. Pigeons that had already made a home there flew about the roof as Percy walked around.

Percy found a big pile of hay. He climbed on top, put some over the top of him and used it for a bed. Percy started to close his eyes and he thought to himself, *it's okay, Percy, this is only the first day.* Then, before he could say goodnight, he fell asleep.

The sun began to rise over grassy hills. All around, you could see the sun shining off the morning dew on the fresh-cut grass. An old cockerel jumped onto the old wooden fence. He forced his chest forward, and with one deep breath, he made the morning cry, 'Cock-a-doodle-doo!' Percy jumped up in shock. He looked around to see what the noise was; he realised that it was outside.

Percy moved the hay away from his body, rubbed his eyes and climbed down from the pile and landed softly on the ground.

He went outside, said 'bye' to the old, little shack and continued to go on his journey. Percy walked along the side of the road and it was all going fine.

Percy was happy and whistling to himself when all of a sudden, from out of the big apple tree, a big, black crow came swooping down. It grasped Percy within its big, claw-like feet. 'Help, help!' Percy shouted, but he was too high for anyone to be able to hear him.

The crow dropped Percy in its big nest made of sticks and mud. Percy thought he was safe until he turned around to see three hatched eggs with three slightly bald, squealing baby crows. Percy screamed. He decided to sit near the edge of the nest in the hope that he would be able to climb to safety.

The mother crow flew away from the nest to get worms for the babies. Percy sat perfectly still. He started to look around for a quick exit. Suddenly, he saw that the nest was in-between two branches, both leading to the centre of the tree. Percy stood up gently and quietly moved around the edge of the nest where one of the branches was. He climbed out and balanced on the branch. He started to walk around the branch, looking foward at all times, trying not to look down. He looked to the side of him and in the distance saw the mother crow soaring back to her nest. She looked at Percy, squawked and began to speed up towards him. For a moment, time seemed to stand still.

Percy couldn't move, then from out of nowhere a sudden boost of courage and energy jumped into Percy. He began to run across the branch and before he knew it, he was on the other side. He took cover behind a few leaves, whilst the mother crow fed her young. Percy took some time to get his breath back. 'That was close', he said to himself, but it wasn't over - the mother crow raised her head and looked towards where Percy had run to. Percy's eyes widened in horror. He didn't have or want time to think, he just got up and looked for a quick way out.

The mother crow hopped onto the branch and began to hop towards Percy, and still Percy struggled to escape. Just the thought of having those tight clutches around his body again made Percy sick to his stomach. Then, for some strange reason, he looked down and saw a hole that seemed to lead to the very bottom of the tree. The mother crow was getting much closer to Percy at this point, then all of a sudden, she flew straight towards him at great speed. Without thinking, Percy closed his eyes and jumped down the hole.

On his way down, Percy could feel the air whooshing past his face. 'Whoo!' he shouted as he sped down the bark of the tree. All of a sudden, the tree seemed to curve and Percy shot off up into the air, landing on a soft patch of grass about a metre away from the tree.

Percy looked up to see the mother crow circling the tree and squawking very loudly, looking for Percy. Percy wiped his forehead. 'It seems this whole outdoors, real life thing can be hard.'

Percy continued his journey and before he knew it, it was night-time again and because he had left the little old shack, he had nowhere indoors to sleep. Instead, he found a hole that had been burrowed in a nearby hill. Percy knew that it wouldn't be comfortable, but still he spent the night.

The next morning, Percy was awoken by the beautiful colours of the sunrise shining in his eyes. His eyes opened, closed, then opened fully. He rubbed his eyes and stretched his arms way out into the air, so that he was fully awake. Percy climbed out of the little hole that he called home for the night, and once again started to walk off to somewhere else.

Percy suddenly found himself on an old, dusty road. It seemed to stretch for miles and miles. Percy didn't think that he could last a journey as long as that, but, being the brave, strong peach that he was, he took a few deep breaths and started to walk along the road.

Percy was now in a world of his own, walking along the middle of the road. He did not hear the cars driving past him, then suddenly, Percy heard a loud honking noise. He looked up to see a great big lorry speeding towards him. He remembered the lorry from the first time he nearly got run over. Percy started to run to the side of the road, but all of a sudden, Percy once again found himself in the clutches of another big bird. Percy's eyes were tightly closed; he thought that he daren't open them, then the next thing he knew, he was lightly placed on the branch of a big, old oak tree. Percy opened his eyes and looked around to see acres of woodland filled with trees of all different sizes. Percy looked beside him to see an old, grey, mother owl.

'Hello there,' said the owl. For a moment, Percy was silent. 'I'm not going to hurt you,' the mother continued.

'Wh-who are you?' asked Percy in a nervous voice.

'I'm Olivia, Olivia the owl,' replied the owl.

'Hi Olivia, my name is Percy. I'm all alone. I ran away because Farmer Green was going to sell me in the market. He took all my brothers and sisters away, but I managed to escape.'

'Oh my,' said Olivia, 'that sounds dangerous,' she continued.

'It is. I've nearly been hurt so many times over the past few days. I was captured by a crow.'

Olivia began to tut. 'Well, I'm glad the mean old crow didn't hurt you, little one. You're safe now.'

'Will you be my friend, Olivia?' asked Percy, hopefully.

Olivia giggled and replied, 'Of course I will.'

Percy smiled to himself, then all of a sudden, a tear trickled down Percy's cheek.

Olivia took Percy under her wing and hugged him. 'What's wrong, Percy?' asked Olivia.

'What should I do, Olivia? I've lost all my family and I cant go back to Farmer Green, but I can't stay out in the wild, it's too dangerous.'

'Well, Percy, maybe that's something you should have thought about before you ran away. You know, maybe we can save some of your family if we fly quick enough.'

Percy's face lit up. 'Really, Olivia?'

'Hop on my back and hold on tight.' Percy did as Olivia said and off they went, flying to the local farmers' market.

When they reached the market place, Percy and Olivia started to search for Farmer Green, but it was very hard because there were lots of people all huddled up together. Percy began to think that it was impossible to find Farmer Green until he heard, 'Five peaches for a pound.'

'That's Farmer Green's voice!' Percy shouted.

Olivia swooped down above Farmer Green's head as he was just about to hand over a bag of peaches to an old man. The bag fell back into the box. Olivia landed on the box. Farmer Green was very angry, then he saw Percy on Olivia's back.

'Is that you, Percy? The one that got away?'

'Yes and I'm very mad at you. You took my brothers and sisters away to sell them!'

Farmer Green's face went from angry to concerned. He then smiled. 'Well, Percy, it would seem that this year hasn't been good and I haven't sold many. In fact, I've sold none from the tree I picked you from.'

'But I saw you sell a lot of peaches to an elderly woman two days ago,' replied Percy.

Farmer Green chuckled. 'Oh my, Percy, they were another farmer's peaches. He asked me to sell his load whilst he went out to pick his daughter, Lucy, up from school.'

Percy's face lit up once more. 'So all my brothers and sisters are still here?'

'Yes, they are Percy,' replied Farmer Green happily. Farmer Green picked up three see-through bags from a box and inside were all of Percy's brothers and sisters.

'Percy!' they all shouted with joy.

Farmer Green opened all three bags and all of the peaches ran towards Percy. Percy ran towards them and they all came together in one giant hug. They all started giggling and smiling.

Percy looked over towards Olivia, who smiled. 'Wait there, guys.' Percy ran over to Olivia and hugged her tightly. 'Please come live with us, Olivia.'

Olivia looked down at Percy. 'I would love to, but it's up to Farmer Green,' replied Olivia.

'Wait here,' said Percy excitedly.

Percy ran up to Farmer Green. Farmer Green looked down at Percy and knelt down so they could see each other properly. 'Farmer Green?' Percy said shyly.

'Yes, Percy?'

Percy cleared his throat and said, 'Would it be OK if my new friend, Olivia the owl, came to live with us?'

For a moment there was no reply. Farmer Green rubbed his black beard, looked at Olivia, then back at Percy and said, 'Of course she can! I would love to have a barn owl.'

Percy jumped for joy and ran over to Olivia. 'Olivia, Olivia! Farmer Green said yes!' Olivia hooted and flew over to Farmer Green, landing on his shoulder.

'Thank you, Farmer Green, for letting me come live on your farm.'

'You're very welcome, Olivia. Come on everybody, back into the van. Let's go home.'

They all got into the van and started to drive down the dusty road. Before they knew it, they were home. Farmer Green walked into the living room and put on the fire. He made everyone a cup of hot chocolate.

'Come on, Percy, tell us about your adventure,' said one of Percy's sisters with great excitement.

Percy smiled, took a quick drink of his hot chocolate and began to speak. 'Hmm, where should I begin?' He began to tell everyone how he escaped from the house and all the troubles he got himself into. But it was getting late, everyone was starting to yawn and before Percy could finish his story, one by one they all fell asleep by the nice, warm fire.

Alysia's Garden

Margaret Holyman

One summer's day, Alysia was outside in the garden of the cottage where she lived with her mummy and daddy. She was wondering what to do today.

The cottage garden was a bit of a mess at the moment. It needed some time spending on tidying it up. The grass was long, the trees were overgrown and the flower borders definitely needed weeding. The reason for this was that Daddy had been working away from home for a while now in Spain and they hadn't lived here in the cottage very long at all before he left and although Mummy had cleaned and decorated most of the rooms inside the house by herself, there was still quite a lot left to do, so the last thing on her mummy's mind at this moment was the garden.

The only thing that was tidy and sturdy was the shed where Alysia kept her toys.

Alysia decided to go and see if any of her friends were in for her to play with. First she called for Hannah, but she wasn't in; she had gone to her grandma's with her mummy, Hannah's daddy told her.

Then she knocked on the door at Brooke's house to see if she wanted to play. There was no answer there at all, so Alysia went straight back home, feeling a little bit sad because she had no one to play with.

Alysia was just bent down picking some daisies from the lawn, when she saw a lovely little rabbit. *It looks so cute,* she thought to herself, *and it doesn't seem frightened of me either.* Alysia kept very still, hoping that the little rabbit didn't run away from her. The thing Alysia noticed most of all was the rabbit's ears; they were very long and floppy. Alysia then thought that if this was a wild rabbit, then surely he or she would have a mummy and daddy and maybe brothers and sisters as well.

Alysia's thinking was quite right because just over the fence at the bottom of the garden, there was a big field that belonged to a farmer named Mr Bell. Then, right at the bottom of Mr Bell's field was a large banking and it was in that very banking that the family of rabbits had burrowed and made their home.

Alysia was now able to see the little rabbit better. It was hopping up and down as if to say *look at me, I'm playing.* Then, at that moment, Alysia's mummy appeared at the cottage door, shouting to tell her that

Daddy was on the phone and wanted to talk to her. Alysia moved then quite quickly and the little rabbit ran off down the garden through the hole in the fence and into the field at the other side.

The little rabbit ran as fast as he could back to the burrow. He had just got back when his mother saw him. She said, 'And where do you think you have been all morning, Floppy? I have been looking all over for you. You were supposed to be going with your father to have a good look around for some food. I was relying on you because just look at that brother of yours, Flopper, he isn't much help at all. He just flops down anywhere and is asleep in no time at all. I can't think of anyone who has to have so much sleep. I couldn't have chosen a better name for him. Now will you please do as I ask, Floppy, and see if you can find any food for us to eat?' Mother rabbit has named this rabbit Floppy because of his large, floppy ears.

Just as father Fred rabbit appeared round a bush, his son, Floppy, ran off in the opposite direction to look for food.

'Oh, there you are, Mother,' said Fred rabbit. 'I haven't found much at all today for us to eat.'

'Don't worry,' said Susie, 'Floppy has just gone to look up in that direction where we haven't been before.' Although mother rabbit's name was really Susie, Fred rabbit always referred to her as 'Mother'.

Fred then asked Mother where Flopper was.

'Need you ask?' said Mother, 'he is in his usual position, fast asleep.' They both started to laugh.

The two youngest rabbits were playing just inside the burrow and were getting in Susie's way while she was doing her jobs. But Susie loved them all so much and was very protective of them. These four rabbits were her babies after all. She had called one of her youngest babies Toffee because he was all one colour, the colour of toffee Susie thought. The other youngest rabbit was called Treacle because Susie thought that he was so small and sweet. He was the smallest of her babies and she liked to keep an eye on her two smallest, even if they did get in her way and make a mess sometimes.

Back at the cottage, Alysia was outside in the garden again after speaking to her daddy on the phone for quite a long time. Just as she was looking around the garden, her mummy came outside to peg out the washing. But Alysia didn't wait for her mummy to get to the washing line, she couldn't wait to tell her about the little rabbit that had been in their garden but who'd run away when she was called to the phone to speak to her daddy.

Alysia was so excited. She was jumping up and down like the little rabbit had done. 'Oh, I wish that I had seen it,' said Alysia's mummy, 'I like rabbits.'

After her mummy had gone back inside the cottage to do some more jobs, Alysia couldn't help wondering if she might get to see the little rabbit again with the long, floppy ears. Oh, she really hoped that she would.

Alysia had just started to play with her doll and pram when she heard her name being called. It was Hannah. She had come back from her grandma's and had come to play. They decided to play shops. Hannah was going to be the shop lady and Alysia was going to the shop with her doll and pram. They played for a short while and then Alysia was just telling Hannah about the little rabbit that had been in the garden, when Brooke came running up to them shouting, 'Alysia, Hannah, hurry up and take these, they are melting.'

Brooke had been shopping with her mummy to the supermarket and had got three ice lollies in her hands. 'Thank you,' said both Alysia and Hannah. They all sat on the lawn to eat them. Alysia then told both Hannah and Brooke about the little rabbit that had been in her garden. All three girls kept their eyes on the hole in the fence, but the little rabbit didn't come back at all that day.

The next morning, Alysia woke up very early. She got out of bed and was washed and dressed in no time at all. She had even brushed her hair and put it in a ponytail. She then went downstairs.

Her mummy said, 'You are up early this morning, love.'

'I know,' said Alysia, 'I want to go outside to see if that little rabbit with the long, floppy ears comes back, Mummy.'

After breakfast, Alysia was off, running down the garden having a good look round. But she didn't see the little rabbit with the long, floppy ears at all. She was just wondering what to play with today, when Hannah and Brooke came into the garden. They too couldn't wait to go outside to play. They were talking about the little rabbit and were wondering if it might be hungry.

Alysia said, 'Just a minute, I can remember Daddy saying to Mummy before he went away, that there were cabbage plants, carrots and I am sure I heard him say lettuce and parsnips as well, all planted behind the shed.'

Then, just as they were going to look round the back of the shed, Alysia saw two rabbits just coming through the broken fence at the bottom of the garden.

'Look,' said Alysia, 'there are two rabbits coming through the hole in the fence.' Hannah and Brooke saw them too. Alysia said, 'It looks like the one that was here yesterday, with the big ears that I told you about. He's come back with another rabbit, look. That one looks half asleep don't you think? Look how slow he is compared to the other one.'

'You are right,' said Hannah and Brooke, 'he does look tired.'

'I bet they are both from the same family,' said Alysia.

'Oh, they are lovely,' said Alysia, Hannah and Brooke all together.

The rabbits were hopping up and down the lawn quite happily now and didn't seem to mind the girls being there watching them. But then, all at once, both rabbits ran off as fast as they could towards the shed. Alysia, Hannah and Brooke watched them and kept very still and quiet.

'Look,' whispered Hannah to Alysia and Brooke, 'they are going round the back of the shed now. I bet they know about the vegetables and lettuce already.'

Brooke said, 'Let's tiptoe quietly round and have a look.'

But the rabbits both ran away. Alysia saw one going through the hole in the fence, but she didn't see where the other rabbit went and neither did Brooke or Hannah. But what Hannah said was right, the lettuce had nearly all been nibbled and so had the carrots. 'Oh no,' said Alysia, then they all started to laugh.

Then Hannah heard her mummy's voice. She was talking to Alysia's mummy, she had come to fetch her. It was time for her dancing lesson. Alysia's mummy wanted her to come inside now as well, it was getting near their teatime. So Alysia said goodbye to her friend, Brooke, and went inside.

Later that night, when Alysia's mummy had tucked her up in bed and kissed her goodnight, she still couldn't get to sleep, no matter how hard she tried. She was thinking about the rabbits and the lettuce and carrots that had nearly all gone before she fell sound asleep.

Alysia's mummy was back downstairs when she realised she had to go outside to put Alysia's pram back in the shed and other toys that Alysia, Hannah and Brooke had got out to play with, and to close and lock the shed door.

But back at the burrow, mother rabbit and father rabbit were very worried when Floppy came home alone. Floppy was trying to explain to his mother what had happened in Alysia's garden, but she wasn't listening and neither was his father.

'Why didn't you come back together like you usually do?' said his father.

'Because I just thought Flopper was behind me. You know how slow he is, he is always running at the back.'

'Yes, Floppy, we know that, but he should be back by now don't you think? We will give him a bit longer, then if he doesn't come home soon, there is only one thing to do. Me and your mother will have to go and look for him while you stay here and keep an eye on Toffee and Treacle so that they don't go missing as well.'

'Alright, Dad,' said Floppy feeling a bit guilty and worried now about his brother, Flopper.

Susie and Fred didn't really know which way to start looking for him.

'He could be anywhere,' said Susie, 'and it's starting to get dark already. Oh, I do hope we find him.'

'Don't worry, love, we'll find him.'

'If only I could believe that, Fred. I bet he is so lost and frightened.'

Susie and Fred looked everywhere, but they did not find Flopper.

'We had better get back to the others now,' said Fred, 'there is nowhere else to look tonight. We'll try again in the morning, Mother.'

When they arrived back at the burrow, the other rabbits were all upset that their mother and father hadn't found Flopper. 'Where can he be?' they all shouted together.

'I don't know,' said Father, 'I only wish I did. Anyway, the only thing to do now is let us all get some sleep.' Then they all settled down for a long night, trying to get some sleep.

The next morning, everyone woke up very early. It was still dark, but they couldn't wait any longer to continue their search for Flopper.

Not too far away, Flopper had just woken, having had a very, very long sleep, *much too long in fact,* he thought to himself. *I know that, so where am I and where is everyone?* He tried to move about, but kept bumping into things and was now becoming very frightened and lost. He had never felt so afraid before in his life. He tried to go back to sleep, but sleep wouldn't come, he was too frightened and cold. He was in fact shivering. Not only was he cold now, he was hungry too and his tummy was rumbling. *Where am I?* He kept thinking, *if only it wasn't so dark.* He jumped around a little more, trying to make out where he was. Then all at once, he landed on something soft and comfortable. He was so tired again now, that he fell fast asleep.

Back at the cottage, Alysia's mummy was downstairs doing breakfast. Alysia was awake now also. She was lying daydreaming when her mummy shouted upstairs, 'Breakfast's ready, love.'

'I'm coming, Mummy,' shouted Alysia.

'What's the matter, Alysia? You are very quiet this morning.'

'I am thinking,' said Alysia.

'I think I only need one guess what you are thinking about. It's those rabbits isn't it?'

'Yes,' said Alysia. 'I have to tell you something. Please don't be cross.'

'Why, what is it?' asked Alysia's mummy.

'Well, you know the lettuce, carrots and vegetables that Daddy planted before he went away to Spain?'

'Yes, what about them, love?'

'Well, the rabbits have eaten a lot of it. Nearly all the lettuce has gone and the carrots have all been nibbled as well.'

'It doesn't matter, love,' said Alysia's mummy. 'To be honest, I had forgotten all about them with being so busy. Well, if the rabbits have eaten them, they haven't been wasted have they, love?' she said. Then she kissed Alysia and they both started to laugh.

After Alysia and her mummy had eaten breakfast, they went outside into the garden. Alysia wanted to play so her mummy had taken the key with her to open the shed so that Alysia could get out her toys. But as Alysia's mummy opened the door, she couldn't believe what she was seeing. On top of the covers in Alysia's doll's pram was a rabbit. It was fast asleep. But not for long because Alysia came running down the path shouting, Look Mummy, there are five rabbits now. Look Mummy, over there!'

Just at that moment, Flopper woke up and jumped as high as he could out of the doll's pram. Alysia and her mummy couldn't stop laughing because the doll's bonnet that was on Alysia's doll, was now on Flopper's head. He ran as fast as his little legs would carry him, with the ribbons of the bonnet blowing in the wind, straight to his family. Alysia and her mummy were still laughing.

Then Alysia said, 'Look how happy he is to see them. Oh no, they are all going now, through the hole in the fence.'

'Don't worry, love,' said Alysia's mummy, 'I am sure they will be back. But one thing's for sure, Alysia, before I lock the shed at night, I think I had better have a good look around for rabbits, especially that lazy one, don't you?'

'Yes,' said Alysia, laughing, 'I do. I just cannot wait to tell Brooke and Hannah what's happened.'

So Many Blueberries

Amy Hagerty

'Let's pick blueberries!' said Claire.

'Great idea,' replied Aunt Judy.

'I'll get the buckets,' said Uncle Frank.

It was a sparkling July afternoon in Maine. All winter, when they were back home, Claire, Aunt Judy and Uncle Frank looked forward to blueberry picking on their summer vacation.

They reached the edge of a field where dozens of wild blueberry bushes flourished. They popped the tasty berries into their mouths.

'We need energy!' said Uncle Frank.

'It looks like the wildlife left plenty for us. We can pack the freezer full,' said Aunt Judy.

'There are so many here, we can have blueberry pancakes every Saturday for the next *three years,*' said Claire.

'Or blueberry scones, or blueberry muffins, or blueberry pies,' added Aunt Judy.

'How about blueberry casserole? Or blueberry pizza? Or blueberry tacos?' joked Uncle Frank.

'Yuck,' said Claire.

'I'll have a blueberry burger, well done, with extra blueberries please, and a side of blueberry nuggets with sweet and sour blueberry dipping sauce,' Aunt Judy suggested before she stuffed a handful of berries into her mouth.

'Extra yucky,' laughed Claire.

They continued picking berries until Uncle Frank stood up, stretched, devoured a fistful of berries and then said, 'For breakfast I'd like a tall glass of fresh-squeezed blueberry juice and a three-egg blueberry omelette, hold the eggs ...' He stopped to eat some more berries.

'I'll have a bowl of New England blueberry chowder for lunch.' After eating another mouthful, smaller than the last one, he went on, 'For dinner I'll have blueberry shish kebabs with marinated blueberries ...' He tossed a few more berries into his mouth.

'If I have room, I'll have a double blueberry soufflé for dessert,' Uncle Frank grinned as he slowly selected one perfect blueberry, closed his eyes and savoured it as if it were the rarest truffle in the world. 'Mmmmmm ... that's an *exquisite* blueberry.'

'Oh Frank, those meals would definitely give you a tummy ache. You'd need a dose of extra strength, blueberry-flavoured antacid before bedtime,' said Aunt Judy.

'I think I'll need something for my aching back too,' said Uncle Frank with a big stretch.

'Hey, break's over. We have too many blueberries to pick!' Aunt Judy said, half-joking.

'Aye, aye, Captain Blueberry,' said Uncle Frank as he saluted her with a blueberry-stained hand and got back to work.

Claire loved seeing her aunt and uncle act goofy, but she was getting tired of crouching, kneeling and bending over to pick blueberries. She didn't want to complain since this adventure was her idea. 'I'll be a good sport and keep the silliness going for the grown-ups,' she said to herself.

Claire thought about blueberry meals, determined to top her aunt and uncle's blueberry creations. Finally, she jumped up and said, 'I have some blueberry ideas! How about a glass of non-fat blueberry milk, scrambled blueberries and *huevos blueberros* for breakfast? For lunch, we'll have diet blueberry sodas and hot, open-faced blueberry sandwiches smothered with blueberry gravy ...' Claire giggled.

'Yucko,' Uncle Frank smiled, scrunched his nose and stuck out his blueberry-coloured tongue.

'For dinner we can have baked, stuffed blueberries, topped with roasted blueberries, Cajun filet of blueberry, and *then* ... Blueberries Jubilee for dessert. How's that?' Claire asked and looked at them eagerly.

'Wow! Bravo!' cheered Uncle Frank as he and Aunt Judy clapped their blueberry-smeared hands.

'Mmmm. All of our talk about food is making me hungry and this work is making me tired. Let's take a break and head back to the cabin for a snack,' said Uncle Frank.

'Anyone up for blueberry fondue?' teased Aunt Judy.

'Enough blueberries!' cried Claire and she covered her face with her hands. This left dark, purple blueberry smudges all over her face.

They wearily trudged back to the cabin, each carrying a heavy bucket filled to the top with blueberries. Claire plopped onto the comfy couch. Aunt Judy stashed the berries into the freezer to be feasted on when they returned home, scrubbed her purplish-blue hands and changed into a fresh shirt. Uncle Frank fixed himself a peanut butter and jelly sandwich and a glass of cold, non-blueberry milk and relaxed in his recliner.

Every time Claire enjoyed blueberry pancakes on frosty mornings back home, she longed for that warm July day when she, Aunt Judy and Uncle Frank had so many blueberries to pick in Maine.

Milligan Shrinkimp

Amanda Hyatt

Milligan Shrinkimp was up to no good - again! Of course, one can't be too judgmental, can one? Not when it comes to imps. After all, it's just not in their nature to behave. What would be the point in being a well-behaved imp? And besides, a shrinkimp's life is short enough as it is - literally. The very tallest shrinkimp baby only ever measured 13¾ centimetres - and by the time he'd learned to hover properly, he was already half a centimetre shorter. This is, of course, the real reason why shrinkimps are so unbelievably badly behaved, by any imp standard. Their lifespan is so brief, they've just got to fit in as much mischief as they possibly can before shrinking to such a small size that they eventually…well, they just vanish, don't they?

Milligan was no exception. Having already lived 5 centimetres of his shrivelling life, he'd decided to make as much use of the remaining 2 as he possibly could. And so we find him, in Mrs Tarquin's lovely garden - or rather, what *used* to be her lovely garden, previously adorned with glorious delphiniums. The ugly slug brawl he'd organised had worked out better than expected and there was really not much left now that you could identify as a flower. Milligan was very pleased with himself. *One has to leave one's stamp on life,* he always thought … and thought … and thought! That was his problem, you see. All thought, no action - not good for a shrinkimp.

Milligan was just about to lapse into yet another millimetre's worth of thinking when a wing-shattering screech sent his ugly little turquoise body hurtling uncontrollably through the air before depositing him very unkindly in a puddle of slug slime, barely an inch from Mrs Tarquin's extremely angry, purple wellies. Unable to hover, Milligan picked himself up as best he could and disappeared quickly behind a flower pot, eager to observe the rest of the proceedings from a position of relative safety.

Mrs Tarquin's face, he noticed with some delight, was now much the same colour as her Wellington boots, her perfect garden full of beautiful delphiniums utterly destroyed. He had chosen the ideal victim. I mean, she was just *too* perfect, wasn't she? More than any shrinkimp could bear. And as for her house - well, imagine this: situated at the end of a very pretty road, the two perfectly square windows at the front of her perfectly square cottage had two sets of the prettiest curtains (imprinted with darling little butterflies and bluebells), each tied back with precisely the same amount of perfectly matching ribbon. The lovely red door with its frieze of delightful robins - and a bell that rang a sweet little tune, opened onto (or, should one say, *used to open onto*) an equally enchanting little garden full of what used to be the most exquisite delphiniums, all growing in perfect clusters and rows, blue on one side, white on the other and pink ones in the middle.

Now, before you comment on how ill you're feeling after reading that revoltingly gushy and quite nauseating description of Mrs Tarquin's *Sweet Pea Cottage*, just think how an imp might feel! *And there's more!* Mrs Tarquin herself, with her pretty face and very smart clothes, was the envy of everyone (except the shrinkimps, of course). She was also the loveliest of ladies; helpful, charming and practical. No one, but no one, would have suspected that she of all people would ever be the target of those naughtiest of naughty imps - or, in this case, just *one* shrinkimp - Milligan! Boy, was he feeling chuffed with himself right now. His squidgy little yellow eyes, sitting either side of the swollen pimple which he called a nose, pulsated in and out and in and out as he watched the sickeningly flawless Mrs Tarquin reduced to a bundle of heaving, blubbering imperfection! Milligan remarked on the fact that in this state even her new dress seemed to have withdrawn and crumpled up in horror at the scene. And what was that crawling up the left purple wellie? A slug! It was a slug! *Oh please look, Mrs Tarquin. Please see it. Please!* thought the evil imp.

No need. Mrs Tarquin's perfect little voice had already found an outlet and was emitting a wail of horror that echoed over the valley with a sound like a cat at the wrong end of a Hoover, bringing the neighbours running to her aid.

'You poor dear!'

'Oh, your poor garden!'

'Where did all those disgusting slugs come from?'

'How did it happen so quickly?'

'Eugh! A slug!'

'Come inside and let me make you some tea.'

The evil imp's nasty turquoise grin widened with every neighbourly comment, showing what was left of his five shrivelled, purple and yellow spotted teeth. Having recovered his hover, he flitted through the open window to enjoy some more of his victim's distress. The sight of biscuit crumbs on the coffee table immediately caught his attention. Unable to resist the opportunity for more *impleness,* he quickly picked them up and hovered over to the piano where he wedged them firmly between the keys, ensuring they stuck nicely. Settling down on an F#, he was pleasantly gloating over his day's successes when ...

'Don't you worry now, Mrs T, we'll have your garden fixed up in no time. No use crying over things like this. It could have been a lot worse, you know ...'

Worse? Could have been *worse*? The very words sent a shudder through Milligan's one-and-a-half centimetre body that knocked him head over wings all the way to the E below. All his efforts, his planning, his dreams to create absolute destruction before the end of his measure and *it could have been worse?*

The sobbing and sighing in the room had abated to an occasional sniffle. 'So soon,' Milligan sighed. He'd hoped it would last much longer than this. Mrs Teapettle was busy lighting some of that revolting stinky stuff that she insisted was 'calming'. Incense, she called it. Milligan watched as the tiny flame snuffed out, a new idea developing inside his shrinking brain. 'That's it!' he cried. 'Flames!' That was what he needed. Oh, he hoped he still had enough length left. Darting through the ghastly smell and out the window once more, he hovered his way up to the chimney top from where he could see the surrounding meadows. Yes, there they were. Milligan was sure he could just see the imps he was looking for flying around in the cornfield. They weren't that difficult to spot - like a puff of red chalk staining the yellow of the corn. Red imps. Fire imps!

If only I could convince General Sparkster to send a few flames down Mrs Tarquin's chimney, Milligan thought, but the shrinkimp need not have worried. The FIA (Fire Imp Army) had been out of action for over two days and were more than delighted to regroup (or, as imps would say, re-cloud) and puff their way immediately towards the much-too-perfect lady's cottage, eager to release a few fiery sparks from their pointed ears.

Milligan was so excited. This was his last chance and he was feeling very proud of himself. Everything was going to work out after all.

... But *wait!* What was that, interrupting his dreams of blazing cottages and smoking wellies? *Ouch! Oof!* Milligan found himself being knocked back and forth and pounded rapidly earthwards by nothing other than ... *raindrops!*

'Noooo,' he cried. 'No! No! No! No! No!' he yelled, flicking his tail up and down (the imp equivalent of stamping one's foot!). Poor Milligan. His last and final plan in droplets! He hadn't banked on rain. Nobody had said anything about rain. Rain - that stuff that puts out fires ... no, he hadn't thought about that. And now ... now it was too late. Only a quarter of a centimetre to go and it looked as though it was going to rain for a lot longer than that. Milligan looked around frantically

as he skitted about, hovering between the drops. What could he do? What could he do? Perhaps ... but no, only an eighth to go ... only ... not even enough time to say 'Good-b ...'

(Pffft!)

The Fairy Tale Story

Jo Hale

'Little Red Riding Hood, where have you been?'
'To the high tower, to paint it bright green
I met up with Cinders and Hansel and Gretel
Who joined in the painting of brickwork and metal
A little while later, Pinocchio turned up
Stirring the paint with his nose, mucky pup!
The colours, they mingled, from one to another
And, one of the Three Pigs mistook his own brother!
For a navy blue statue - oh, how we laughed!
When Buttons joined in, and then had to be bathed!
He splashed and he lathered and threw water about
Causing lots of merriment, laughing and shouts
But, Billy Goat Gruff, he got in a mood
When, soggy and messy, got the basket of food
Then, behind the tower, an orchard we found
Where lovely red apples had fallen to the ground
We munched and we feasted - each filled our belly
Then Humpty Dumpty discovered some wobbly jelly
That was safe, undamaged, in the soppy wet hamper
Though the rest of the food, it was left slightly damper!
Wandering along, was Little Bo Peep
She told us she'd passed an Ogre - the creep
Who took about twenty and four of her lamb
He thought they were bacon, or honeydew ham!
Despairing, was she - oh, what could she do?
Her flock numbers dwindling - missing a few
Rapunzel suggested we all go along
To see the Ogre, and sing it a song'
'A song!' said the Three Bears, 'What good would that be?'
The Ogre, at us, he would laugh with such glee
'That is the point,' said Rapunzel with flair
And flamboyantly, tossed back her long, golden hair
'If he thinks we are funny and laughs at us so
It will give us a chance to distract him, you know
And, when he's not looking, all of us will
Grab hold of a lamb each and run for the hill.'
'Great idea,' said the Woodcutter, 'I think it might work.

'Yes,' said Goldilocks, cos that Ogre's a berk!
Remember that time when the Gingerbread Man
Told him a joke about a new hunting ban?'
'Yes!' laughed Tom Thumb, 'I remember it well
The Ogre was aghast - and over he fell,
Kicking and screaming and hammering his fist
On the ground, with such fury - you all get the gist?'
The Pied Piper remembered another such time
When the Ogre was fooled, whilst committing a crime
'He was fishing for fairies along the creek riverbank
Took fright at his own reflection, fell in, and then sank!'
Puss in Boots, passing by, said with such glee
'Hello there, Ogre, in some trouble are thee?'
And the Ogre, he roared and he spat at the cat
Who ran away sniggering, whilst waving his hat
At a passing stagecoach, with Prince Charming inside
Puss in Boots wanted to gossip, whilst hitching a ride.
'And, there was that time,' said Old Mother Hubbard,
'When he wore those new clothes, which he stole from
                                    my cupboard.'
'We remember,' said the Blind Mice, 'he thought he looked swell
But, the clothing was ladies, he just couldn't tell!'
'Yes, well,' said Bo Peep, 'all this talking is fine
But, can we get on and recover what's mine?'
'Yes,' we all said, 'we must go without haste
For the Ogre will be hungry - there's no time to waste.'
We found the Ogre teasing Quasimodo,
The poor lad was making excuses to go.
He's very shy and gets picked on a lot
And, the Ogre's a bully, he doesn't care a jot,
About whom he offends - he just thinks it's funny,
Robin Hood, Mother Goose or the Easter Bunny.
They've all stood his taunting and teasing, it's true,
Ugly Duckling included, and Little Boy Blue,
But, times were a-changing, we were to fight back
For there was that beanstalk that was grown by Jack,
Who would climb it and tell the Giant at the top
That the Ogre was mocking them, and it had to stop.
So Jack climbed to the top of the green stalk
Where the Giant sat dozing, all big, brawn and balk,
'Jack!' he cried, 'Hello my dear fellow!
Grab a seat! Take a pew! Sit down and mellow!'

'I'd love to, you know, but I'm here for a favour
I really should get back and really not waiver.'
'What troubles ye so?' The Giant did frown,
So, Jack told the story of the Ogre in town.
The Giant, he listened and did not like much
Of what he was hearing of this Ogre and such,
'Rumplestiltskin did mention him on his last visit
But talked of the Ogre's clothes, saying they were exquisite
And Sleeping Beauty did talk of it too
Though she just kept yawning and wanting the loo.
Please rest assured, my good friend Jack
You go tell the others that I'll sort out that hack
I'll come down just as soon as I've eaten
Then I'll be heavier and the Ogre will be beaten.'
Climbing back down, Jack noticed the others
Had gathered around the stalk, dads, kids and mothers
To hear just what the Giant had said
Before going home to put the children to bed.
As Jack was explaining, the Giant appeared
All mighty (and clean!) - a sight to be feared,
In search of the Ogre, the Giant he went
And saw Little Jack Horner, by a tree, his head bent,
'Ah, Jack, me lad, whatever's the matter?'
'It's the Ugly Sisters, they just keep getting fatter,
They take away my lovely plum tarts
And eat them in front of me! Oh, they have such cold hearts.'
'You should cheer up, young Little Jack Horner,
For there is the Muffin Man, over in the corner
He's measuring the Ugly Sisters around each their waist
And the tape measure's stretching! Oh, just look at each face!
That'll teach them to take your tarts of plum
Those tasty treats have left those sisters really glum!
You won't have any more trouble, young Jack
You see if I'm not right, those sisters won't be back!
I'm off now to find this terrible Ogre bully
And find out his problem, oh yes, quite fully
For he has been terrorising you poor town folk
And I won't have it, and this isn't a joke.
I'll sort him out, oh yes, good and proper
Messing with you lot, oh, he'll come a cropper
And what's that I spy, he has hold of ole Sneezy
Also, Bad Wolf, and he's made them quite wheezy.

Stop that you Ogre, you foul, mean heejee,
Put down those creatures, and just leave them be
And, leave this town, for I rule this land
And I don't take to strangers getting the upper hand.
This is my territory and it always will be
We now all live together in perfect harmony,
And I'm bigger than you, so you run along
Far away from here, cos you don't belong,
And if you backchat me, or put up a fight
I'll sort you out properly, with my muscle and might,
For I am the bigger one between you and I
And I know for certain that I'll make you cry.
So give back those lambs and you will save face
Be heading off now, cos you're a disgrace
Leave here right now and don't turn around
And never return here, or you'll see what you're bound.'
So away walked the Ogre, his silly head bowed
By the increasing cheering of the gathering crowd
'Three cheers for the Giant!' Their noise it was loud
For the Giant, their hero, they were so very proud.
Red Riding Hood, tell me, this all happened today?
'Oh yes, as I told you, 'tis the fairy tale way!'

Timmy The Tugboat

Stuart Barns

Timmy pulled up his anchor with a great big heeeave ... ready for another day in Jollyship Bay. The sun was beaming down onto Timmy's hot deck and his newly painted underbelly of bright red and blue made him the proudest boat on the water.

Just then the harbourmaster was waving frantically and shouting, 'Quick, quick! We need your help, Timmy. A ship's in trouble, take a look.'

Timmy popped his head over the harbour wall and could see an enormous ship tilting to one side not far from the shore of Jollyship Bay. The big ship was puffing and wheezing with the strain and blowing steam hard and fast from his funnel as he tried in vain to stay upright.

'Ooohh, someone help, someone help!'

'Oh, shivering starfishes. On my way harbourmaster!'

With a huge splash, Timmy darted through the water with the speed and grace of a racing sea horse, weaving in and out of the moored fishing boats on the way.

'I'm coming, I'm coming Mr Ship,' Timmy shouted at the top of his voice.

As Timmy got closer and closer, the tall ship towered above him, blocking out the golden morning sun.

'Oh my! You're so big ... and ... heavy looking.'

The big ship groaned and creaked. 'My cargo is oil drums, Timmy and they are very heavy. I've hit a big rock and the hole in my side is letting in water. Unless you help me, the oil might spill into the water and Jollyship Bay will become polluted.'

'Oh no,' said Timmy. 'We won't let that happen. What can I do? Wait a minute, I've got an idea!'

Night Ride

Ivy Allpress

Friday afternoon again. How quickly it seemed to come around.

Friday afternoon was when the boy, accompanied by his mother and grandma, went to the shopping centre to do the weekend shopping.

He was not terribly keen on this part of the expedition, but it did not really bother him all that much, there was usually a treat involved for him, also he had an escape route. The grown-ups did not want a discontented boy trailing round after them, so he was allowed to go to his favourite place, which was a garden - a peaceful spot centred in the busy parade of shops and stores and was much appreciated at lunchtime by the busy workers. There was also a pond with fountains which added to its attractions.

The boy's favourites were the bronze statues. They were larger than life-size and the boy loved climbing all over them.

One of the statues was a boy on a bike and he had a mischievous look about him, rather like the boy himself.

There was also a modern looking girl walking her dog, a young man carrying a toddler on his shoulders and a couple with a baby in a buggy. He happily climbed all over them, imagining all sorts of adventures, but his favourite was definitely the boy on the bike. He looked as though he hadn't a care in the world and it naturally attracted the boy.

The shopping being completed, his mother and grandma came to collect him for the journey home, which was quite pleasant as he received his reward for keeping out of their way while they shopped.

It was dusk when he found himself in the shopping centre. He had no idea how he had got there. He always thought that it shut at a certain time in the evening. He went straight to the garden and to his amazement, the bronze statues were walking about. The girl with the dog was walking it round the pond, the couple with the buggy and the man with the toddler set off in opposite directions and the boy on the bike gave him a knowing wink and indicated that he should get on the bike with him. The boy jumped up and perched on the bar and *whoosh,* away they went at great speed around the pond a few times, startling the girl walking her dog and then out through the doors of the shopping centre which opened as if by magic. They rose up into the night sky. He felt almost as if they were riding with the stars which were

 New Fiction - Fairy Tales For Little Imps

now coming out. The wind was ruffling his hair and he looked down and saw the whole town spread out before him. He could see the roads, busy with the rush-hour traffic, the black, winding river snaking along and the straightcut canal with its colourful, long boats where he went fishing with his father on Sunday mornings. There was his school - he would have something to tell them on Monday morning. He saw the church and the weathervane on top of the steeple. He felt he could almost touch it as they rushed past.

He saw places that he knew and some places that he hadn't realised were there at all. He would certainly have to go exploring the countryside where he lived, especially that old castle which looked grim but very exciting. He felt that now he could map the whole country, it seemed much brighter now with the arrival of a big, yellow, harvest moon. Then he noticed that the sky seemed to be getting lighter. He realised that it must be daylight coming and began to wonder how he was going to get home.

He need not have worried. Suddenly, he was back in the garden. The other statues were back on their plinths and he realised that his great adventure was over. He whispered a hurried, 'Thank you' to the boy on the bike and then landed with a bump on his bedroom floor. He looked around utterly bewildered. His mother came in the room.

'Fallen out of bed again? I'll have to get you some bed boards.'

He did not mind about the bed boards. He would easily take them down if she ever got them. He was puzzled about the night's adventure. It could not possibly be a dream. It was all so real. He could remember all of it, the walking statues and most of all the boy on the bike. He felt he was his friend.

The Friday expedition came round again and the boy went straight to the garden. The statues all stood primly on their plinths and the boy was perched on his bike. The boy climbed up and perched beside his friend and whispered, 'Thank you,' once more, but there was no response. He looked into his eyes, but they were expressionless, just bronze shapes. The adventure was well and truly over, but he could not accept it yet - the vividness of it all, he would never forget it and he never told anybody about it. It was his own private adventure, too precious to be shared with anyone else.

He continued to visit the statues until other interests took over, but he never forgot his bronze bike-riding friend and their exciting night ride. Even when he was grown up and moved away from the town, the memory lingered on in the back of his mind. Was it real, or a figment of an over-active imagination, or had it been after all a wonderful dream?

Adventures With Forest Friends

Lorna Tippett

The snow came early on Ashdown Forest this year, covering everything with its fascinating coat of white, making everywhere look very beautiful, in fact, ready for a story to be told.

As you know, Ballyhoo, the friendly badger, lives there with his many friends. Possibly his favourite friend is Robert the rabbit who you may remember is always worrying about the time and is constantly looking at his pocket watch to check the time. His immediate reaction on checking is to say how late he is and suddenly, he disappears, only to reappear in the most unexpected places.

Ballyhoo, the friendly badger, began making his way through the forest to meet Robert the rabbit, because they had decided to get all their forest friends together to have a gathering in the snow and practise tobogganing. They thought it might be a good idea to offer a prize for the contestant who travelled the fastest down the slope. In the Hollies, Robert the rabbit suddenly spotted Ballyhoo and gave him a friendly wave.

'I wondered if you would manage to get here as the snow is so deep, especially at Friend's Clump.'

After they had exchanged a friendly greeting to one another, they made their way towards the Enchanted Glade where all the animals were going to meet. Suddenly, Ballyhoo called, 'Oh, look over there. Do you see what I see? Oh, look in that tree, it's Mr and Mrs Colman's beautiful cat, Andrea.'

'Oh my goodness,' cried Robert the rabbit, 'she is a pedigree. Did you know that?'

'No,' said Ballyhoo.

'Oh yes,' said Robert the rabbit, 'she is what is called a Rag Doll.'

'Well, well,' said Ballyhoo.

Robert the rabbit called out to Andrea to ask if she was alright.

'No,' came a pathetic little whimper. 'I am so frightened. I was up here when the snow came and I just couldn't get down. Now the snow is so deep, I would sink in the snow and no one would find me.'

'Never you mind,' said Ballyhoo, the friendly badger, 'we will help you. Now, if you jump onto my back, Robert the rabbit will lift you off and carry you to the Enchanted Glade. You can come and have some fun with us.'

After the rescue of Andrea from the pine tree and landing securely on Ballyhoo's back, then being lifted off by Robert the rabbit and being securely tucked in his pocket with just enough room to peek from the pocket flap to see everything that was going on, the trio set off for the Enchanted Glade.

By now, the snow was very deep, in fact Ballyhoo and Robert the rabbit began to get a little worried because the sky looked very grey, as if any time there would be another fall of snow.

'Do you think we should shelter? I do,' said Andrea. She was feeling rather uncomfortable stuffed in Robert the rabbit's pocket, although under the circumstances there was nothing else that could be done.

'OK, let's rest under that bush.'

As it happened, there appeared to be a dry patch which was ideal for a shelter from the oncoming snow. They made their way into the enclosure and began to settle down. Immediately Andrea jumped from Robert the rabbit's pocket and began to explore. She loved searching for interesting things to do and would you believe, she discovered a tiny little hole just big enough for her to scrabble through. In a moment, she had pushed her way through and was in a little area like a little nest. In a corner was a little bundle of straw. She wandered over and with her paw began to tap the straw, with her little nose getting nearer and nearer. Suddenly, a little nose peeped out, a nose much smaller than Andrea's.

'Oh dear,' said a little voice, 'you have woken me up from my winter sleep.'

'I am sorry,' said Andrea, 'but I am just sheltering from the heavy snow and I found my way in here. May I ask your name?'

'Of course. My name is Harvey. In the normal state of affairs, I am afraid I would run away from you as you are a cat and you would swallow me whole.'

'Oh no I wouldn't,' said Andrea. 'I only play with mice. Because I'm a pedigree, I have to have special food and would never eat a mouse anyway. I am very pleased to meet you. My name is Andrea. I am with Ballyhoo, the friendly badger and Robert the rabbit. They are sheltering from the snow. Come out and meet them.'

'I am rather shy you know,' said Harvey.

'Oh, come on,' said Andrea. 'I am sure they would love to meet you. In fact, I think they will ask you to come and join us. Come on, it will be fun.'

Following Andrea, Harvey soon found himself in the clearing where Ballyhoo and Robert the rabbit were waiting, wondering where Andrea had disappeared too.

'This is Harvey harvest mouse,' said Andrea.

'I expect he was asleep,' said Robert the rabbit.

'Well, yes he was.'

'As I thought,' said Ballyhoo, the friendly badger. 'Well, would you like to come with us to the Enchanted Glade? We are going to play on toboggans.'

'Yes please,' replied Harvey.

'When it's safe, you can climb into my other pocket,' said Robert the rabbit, 'as Andrea has one of them to ride in.'

'Thank you,' said Harvey, giving a little squeak of pleasure.

After a while, Ballyhoo, the friendly badger, pushed the bushes aside to see how things were as regards to travelling to the Enchanted Glade. To his surprise, Fredrick the fallow deer was peering through the bushes at Ballyhoo.

'Hello,' said Fredrick, 'do you want a lift on my back?'

'Yes please,' said Ballyhoo. 'We are going to the Enchanted Glade to play on toboggans. You can join us if you would like to, it promises to be good fun.'

Of course, Fredrick the fallow deer was thrilled to be asked.

After Ballyhoo, the friendly badger, and Robert the rabbit, with Andrea in one of his pockets and Harvey harvest mouse in the other had climbed onto Fredrick's back, they set off for the Enchanted Glade in the deep snow.

After they had passed the Pylons, a picnic area, and were heading towards Shadows, another popular picnic area, Fredrick stumbled and started falling. Of course, Ballyhoo and Robert the rabbit fell off too and started rolling, rolling. Poor Andrea and Harvey, they wondered what was going on, what was happening.

When they finally finished rolling, Ballyhoo called to see if everyone was alright. As it happened, because of the snow which offered a soft landing, no one was hurt. Andrea called from Robert the rabbit's pocket, 'Can I come out now?'

'Yes, yes, out you come,' called Robert, 'but take care because I think we have landed in Smugglers' Trail. Although the snow is not so deep, you still have to take care.'

'Don't forget me,' squeaked Harvey. He too wanted to leave the comfort of Robert the rabbit's pocket. He wanted to know what was going on. It was decided Harvey would sit amongst Andrea's fur and ride on her back. Andrea thought this a splendid idea and very soon they were all on their way; Ballyhoo the friendly badger, Robert the rabbit, Andrea the fluffy pussycat, Harvey harvest mouse and Fredrick the fallow deer.

After a while it was decided Andrea would be better on Fredrick's back with Harvey, nestled amongst her fur. Everyone then moved much faster. They all found it rather exciting, walking along Smugglers' Trail and hoping very much they wouldn't meet any forest nastiness. As they made their way, Andrea noticed little, sparkling jewels on the branches of the trees and bushes. She called out to Fredrick to slow down, she wanted to touch them. Stretching her little paw, she managed to reach one and immediately it disappeared.

Harvey called to her, 'It's water, Andrea, it's from the snow and ice.'

Andrea thought this was wonderful and managed to catch some as they passed, on the end of her nose. She and Harvey thought this was great fun. In fact, Andrea dropped some over Harvey. He laughed, although he thought it was jolly cold.

Soon they passed Smugglers' Trail, without meeting anyone too nasty and of course breathed great sighs of relief whilst entering Gorsey Down, where here the snow hadn't settled too heavily, so they managed to make good progress. Suddenly, without warning, Robert the rabbit took his watch from his waistcoat pocket. He glanced at it and cried, 'I'm late, I'm late!' and in a flash he'd vanished.

Andrea and Harvey were a little bit scared. 'What happened?' they cried.

'Don't worry about Robert,' said Ballyhoo, 'he will surprise you later.'

After pausing at Gill's Lap North, Fredrick suggested Ballyhoo climbed on his back with Andrea and Harvey, they would make even better progress.

'Good idea,' said Ballyhoo and away they went, almost flying.

Fredrick the fallow deer was known for his good ideas and his quiet, unassuming ways.

'Here we are,' said Fredrick, 'the Enchanted Glade.'

They went through the entrance to meet all the forest friends and much to the surprise of Andrea and Harvey, but not Ballyhoo or Fredrick, who should welcome them but none other than Robert the rabbit. He gave them a huge, whiskery smile and encouraged them to try some of the delicious snacks he had prepared for them to enjoy.

Before the competition began, which they had now decided to have just outside the Enchanted Glade as there were some lovely long slopes, just right for tobogganing, Ballyhoo called all the young animals together: Martha mouse and her family of five, Bill badger and his son, Bertie, Frank fox and his litter of three, Freda, Felicity and Tommy,

Sarah, Shirley and Susan from the flock of sheep. He suggested they build an enormous snowman. Whilst the others used large barks of the trees as their sledges to race down the snow slopes. The snow had actually stopped falling now, so conditions were perfect to begin.

Everyone was getting very excited. Ballyhoo said he would go first to show the others there was nothing to be frightened about. Away he went, lying on his tummy (he liked showing off a bit). Robert the rabbit had given him a little push which Ballyhoo didn't seem aware of. Everyone shouted and cheered him as he sped down the snowy slope. Of course, he loved this enthusiasm of support. Suddenly, the enthusiasm waned a little because Ballyhoo hit Malcolm mole's house and his sledge went on its side. Ballyhoo had to hold on tight, but as luck would have it, he made his way to the bottom of the slope and rolled into the snow, laughing merrily. He called to his friends standing on the top of the slope, encouraging them to come on down, it was wonderful. Robert the rabbit thought it might be an idea if he followed, with Andrea and Harvey harvest mouse with him. Robert placed himself carefully on the sledge, told Andrea to sit between his legs and Harvey would nestle in-between Andrea's paws. This worked beautifully and away they sped, laughing, squeaking and purring merrily all the way, missing Malcolm mole's house. They reached the bottom and fell into Ballyhoo's arms, having thoroughly enjoyed the ride. Ballyhoo called for the other friends to follow and have some fun. Soon all the forest friends were speeding down the snowy slope, two and three times, having a cool, cool time. Fredrick the fallow deer stayed on the top of the slope, making sure everyone knew what to do and of course, more refreshments had to be arranged, which Fredrick enjoyed preparing.

When the fun and excitement had come to a close, Andrea and Harvey harvest mouse were feeling tired. It was decided they would return to Robert the rabbit's pocket and he, with Ballyhoo the friendly badger and Fredrick the fallow deer, would journey home together.

Not forgetting the prize, Ballyhoo and Robert the rabbit thought it would be a splendid idea if they all went to the Ashdown Forest hotel and enjoyed a day at the spa being pampered. Everyone was overjoyed with the idea and just longed for the day to come when they would all meet up again. Already Andrea the fluffy pussycat and Harvey harvest mouse were tucked up inside Robert the rabbit's pockets, fast asleep, dreaming of a day at the spa.

The Cave Of The Dragon

Pamela Harvey

The sky was troubled. The orange streaks were back. The sun was hidden for several minutes behind a cloud. Doreen looked up, worried. Only since the coming of the fireballs and the winds had the sun appeared to her and her family and friends. It had been a wonderful, almost scary thing to see the bright ball in the heavens where clouds had always been. You couldn't look at it either. Even Doreen's mother had shielded her eyes. Now Doreen frowned. The clouds were back and a sharp, cold wind blew. She shivered, in spite of her thick skin with its strong scales. She looked down at her body. She was still only a little dinosaur really, but every day she seemed to grow a little bit and she had felt the welcome warmth of the sun that dispelled the mist that over recent months had crept in mornings and evenings when the clouds were thickest. Now it was coming in again and the wind had picked up. Mother said the clouds and this new troubling wind did not go together.

Suddenly, Doreen jumped. A sizzling-hot pellet had landed right next to her. It set fire to some of the long grass, but fizzled out gradually because of the grass being very damp. The clouds were making everything dark. Then another dazzling fireball, this time much bigger, seared its way overhead. Doreen lowered her head. She looked around her wildly. Her friends had gone home; her mother was probably waiting for her to come home for tea as well. Doreen suddenly, in spite of her growing panic, felt hungry. The soft, chewy leaves of the big cycad tree were delicious to dinosaurs when stewed, and the warm brew that Mother made from the grasses …

Another fireball, this time even bigger and in the darkened sky, the growl of thunder. Doreen felt panic giving her wings, almost as if she had grown them like some strange dinosaurs called dragons. She charged through the long grasses and then - *bump!*

'Ouch! Ugh!' A low, loud voice, something like the thunder, only less powerful, stopped Doreen in her tracks. At the very next moment, as she slowed down a bit, she found herself tumbling over a large object she had not had time to see, but which continued to groan and protest. She did not want to look back, she just wanted to get home because she could hear another sizzling fireball not far behind and the sky was starting to rain ash, which stung her despite her hard, shiny, scaled armour. The object that had led to her stumbling suddenly reached out and grabbed her so that she fell over. Protecting herself, she looked round. Yes, it was a human - one of those hairy, broad-faced, ugly little creatures that were so rare, they were prized by anyone who captured them, but who were fierce in their pathetic way, though no match for even a very small dinosaur.

'Oogh!' said the human, pulling hard at Doreen's leg. She wriggled, but could not detach herself. She began to get angry and lashed out at him, but she was a kind little dinosaur and didn't really want to hurt him. He was quite a lot smaller than her.

'Stop it!' she ordered him. Then she noticed the anxious look on his wide face. His big teeth were clenched, but then more sounds came from his mouth. He let go of Doreen and with one of his long arms, pointed to a cave not far away. Then he pointed to the sky. The clouds were black now. It was getting dark far too soon. But every few seconds it seemed, another flaming pellet or ball came towards the ground. Fires were beginning to start, even on damp grass, so constant were the missiles from the sky. Doreen realised the human was indicating shelter - for both of them. As he saw she understood, the boy let go of Doreen and they both scurried towards the cave.

They entered a dark, but welcome shadow. Everywhere was damp and the only light came from more fireballs landing just outside. In one of these flares, Doreen saw that in front of them was a very long passage. It wound towards the end part, that was all she could see, and disappeared into the greater darkness. The boy, she could just make out, was rubbing a shiny object on his leg. It was some kind of rough disc, reddish in colour. He held it up for her to see in the flashing light. Completely startled, Doreen saw another dinosaur staring at her with a scared expression. But there was no other dinosaur anywhere near. She visibly jumped.

'Magic!' said the human, but Doreen did not know even the very few words of his language. These humans made themselves understood with each other, by signs, by touching, and sometimes by sounds that were - what Doreen did not understand - an attempt at words. This was apparently a very important word because the boy repeated it again for her benefit. He looked very solemn when he did so. He turned the object towards himself. Another boy showed up in it. Doreen was by now extremely uneasy and, but for the threat outside, would have run out. He was grunting and trying to find words and then, suddenly; it dawned on her. Both the other dinosaur and the other boy came into the darkish, but definite picture. Doreen had never seen a mirror in her life, but she had finally got the message! She was a clever little dinosaur with an intelligence which would one day quite outsmart most humans. But this boy was clever too. Doreen took a good look at him as he grinned broadly. Yes, surely she recognised him. He wasn't bad looking either. Of course, all humans must look alike and Doreen had only ever seen one before once. He had been a half-grown one too and he had taken her on a very strange journey on a flying stone he had called 'magic'. She spoke to him in dinosaur language, but he seemed to understand.

'You are - Ugh-Ogh?'

'Yes!' The boy nodded very definitely. 'I remember you, too, Doreen the dinosaur and you've grown. But I have too.' He flexed his muscles and all the dark ginger hairs on them stood up and bristled. He was getting powerful shoulders, Doreen thought. She realised something else, she only understood an occasional word, but her thoughts seemed to combine with his. Mysterious, but exciting and in this situation, helpful. For outside it seemed a storm had started. Thunder growled like a hungry tyrannosaurus-rex, only more so! Lightning flashed, so that the cave was lit up and then another sizzling-hot fireball bounced right into the cave. This time they both jumped.

Doreen's mind was getting a strange message - and it concerned the long passage in front of them and the curve, around which she could not see in the light from outside. But the boy had realised something else. Someone - human - had been here before. There were their splayed footprints on the ground where it was not damp, but sandy or dusty, and they had dropped an object, a wooden object that he reached out and grasped. It was - yes, a torch. It was almost falling apart, but his strong hands curled around it. A fiery pellet danced into the cave and quick as the lightning, he pushed the torch against it and suddenly, they had a light that shone all around the cave and in front of them, too.

Ugh-Ogh guided Doreen along the passage until they came almost up to the curving part. But Doreen had noticed how the wind had come in and now seemed to be blowing fiercely in *front* of them ... It stung her face and even Ugh-Ogh winced. It even seemed to get into and under her skin, so that it pulled. She felt she was being drawn into the darkness of the cave. She stood stock still, while the wind blew silently over her scales and made Ugh-Ogh's dark, strong hair stand on end, so that he began to look a bit like a small dinosaur!

Then, from around the corner, blew another wind. This was hot and Doreen knew it was the breath of a very large dinosaur. Suddenly, he appeared, huge, scaly and with big nostrils flaring. In the dark, the fire from them seemed even stronger than the torch. Doreen was not too scared. Mother had told her many tales of their ancestor dragons who looked scary, but were really wise and could be helpful.

The dragon's nose and mouth still breathed fire, but he spoke. Doreen tried hard not to be afraid, especially when she saw Ugh-Ogh was about to run back, taking his torch with him. She held on to him tightly, in trying to reassure him finding her own fear easing a little. But not enough …

'This is a forbidden place!' said the big dragon. 'Especially to humans. Only the very wise, and those who have learned from us, can come here. It is nearly round the bend in the passage, where it is a secret passage that leads to …'

'The land of dragons, giants and fairies,' said Doreen, finding her voice. But she saw a change in Ugh-Ogh's expression. His teeth no longer chattered in fear. Instead, he held up the round, reddish-gold, burnished object that had shown Doreen their reflections. The dragon nodded and looked at him keenly, but with interest. Even a little respect.

'You are young!' he thundered, 'but already you begin to understand.' And Ugh-Ogh seemed to understand the meaning of his words too, using human language as far as that was at all possible.

The boy held up the mirror. Doreen saw that it showed an angle of the path ahead that neither of them could actually see because of the curve and also because the path seemed to disappear, swallowed up in mist … but in the mirror there was no mist. Just a continuation of the path …

'Where few humans have trod,' bellowed the dragon, but a bit more kindly. 'Unless they are given strength by us, or they have come to the end of their time on what you call, Earth.'

'That is death!' Doreen's voice was scarcely above a whisper.

'Exactly!' answered the big dragon.

She didn't understand Ugh-Ogh's next words, but they clearly implied he did not want to die. At least, not for a very, very long time. Doreen agreed with him telepathically. She looked imploringly at the dragon. 'We are both little,' she pleaded.

The dragon's big lips curled in a secret smile, a half smile, as if part hidden like the path ahead. 'You already tread the path,' he said, 'but you are afraid to set your feet down any further, although until you fight the strong wind here, you need not think you will not get back. All worlds are one, really. It is only that sometimes we cannot see the path ahead anywhere, though it is everywhere …'

'We must get back! I think the storm outside is lessening,' Doreen found the excuse. Her little legs were beginning to shake, then the boy's shivering fingers suddenly loosened their hold on his torch while still managing to firmly grasp his mirror. For a moment, outside the lightning no longer flashed; the fireballs seemed to stop in their furious dance. It was dark, except for the glowing light of the dragon's body and the fire from his nose and mouth. It showed up his huge, multicoloured scales that were still just a bit like Doreen's. The boy swung his mirror in an even wider arc. Suddenly, it too glowed and ahead of them they saw even more of the passage. You could see the light - of the other entrance. But it lit the path.

'In the land of dragons, giants, fairies and wizards!' whispered Doreen, as suddenly she lost her balance and stumbled forward, just towards the bend in the secret path. The boy, grabbing his torch, reached out to her too, but the torch would no longer light. The only lights in the area now were from another world ... as there the sun was shining and between them and it, the dragon's body stood huge and wreathed in its own fire ...

I'm treading the path, thought Doreen, *and I don't want to. I want to go home!*

The dragon's lips once more curled in that haunting smile. 'You will, this time,' he said softly. 'But you have learned something today, haven't you? I know you have. Neither of you will ever forget and when, in many years from now, in the future, the sky will be filled with fireballs and one big fireball that will eat up a lot of the whole world, you will know where to find refuge - and escape. You will lead all other creatures to this place, and there are many other places like it, where they will find somewhere to hide in the many side entrances and passages that lead to other parts of the world - or, you will guide them through onto the path into the secret world we guard ... where there is no actual death and where the hidden path leads to another sun shining in a new dawn for everyone ...'

Doreen and Ugh-Ogh suddenly found themselves landing with a bump outside the cave, and the sun was shining. Doreen waved to her mother, who was coming towards them.

Pollyanna's World!
Pollyanna Goes To
The Supermarket

Anne-Marie Howard

Today is Saturday and every Saturday Pollyanna goes shopping with her mum, dad and older brother, Charlie, at their local supermarket. Pollyanna loves going shopping, she likes to put the vegetables into bags, unlike Charlie who absolutely hates shopping unless it's for toys or computer games.

'I want to go to the cinema!' said Charlie grumpily.

'Charlie, you know it's supermarket day today, now please be good!' said Dad.

Pollyanna was very excited. 'Mum,' said Pollyanna, 'can I put the coin into the trolley for you?'

'Yes, of course you can, darling,' answered Mum.

'Goodie.'

'Goodie,' said Charlie to Pollyanna, just loud enough for her alone to hear. Charlie looked miserable. Pollyanna put the coin into the trolley and walked happily in through the supermarket doors with Mum and Dad. Charlie walked in behind them with his arms crossed, dragging his feet heavily along the floor.

'Come along, Charlie,' called Dad.

Mum and Dad stopped in the middle of the grocery aisle and waited for Charlie to catch up.

Pollyanna just loves to use her imagination. Pollyanna picked up a packet of runner beans. 'Umm, runner beans, she said to herself. Suddenly she imagined herself running the marathon alongside some of the finest runner beans in the country.

'Come along, Pollyanna,' called Mum.

The next aisle was very cold: it was the frozen food section. Mum reached for the fish fingers. Pollyanna smiled, she found herself sitting in a beauty parlour having a manicure next to a beautiful lady fish. 'What lovely nails you have, Miss Fish,' said Pollyanna.

'Why thank you, young lady,' said the lady fish.

Just then, Dad asked, 'Are you daydreaming again, Pollyanna?'

'Oh no, Dad,' she said, nearly jumping out of her skin.

'Yes you were, liar!' smirked Charlie. Pollyanna turned her nose up at Charlie and turned to look inside the freezer on the opposite side of the aisle.

'French fries!' Pollyanna read.

'Bonjour!' said the French fries.

'Oh hello, Fries, she answered politely as if it were perfectly normal to talk to a bag of chips! Then she skipped off happily to join Mum, Dad and Charlie.

'Mum, can I have some sweets?' asked Charlie.

Mum said, 'Choose a sweet but you can't have it until after your lunch!'

'Alright,' agreed Charlie.

Pollyanna noticed one of Charlie's coat buttons on the floor and so she picked it up. 'Charlie, you've lost a button!' Pollyanna explained, holding it up high.

'Put it in my pocket!' he said and Pollyanna popped it into his pocket. Just to be on the safe side, Pollyanna put a pack of chocolate buttons into Mum's trolley in case he lost anymore. Dad reached for the milk and a bottle of milkshake toppled over. Luckily Pollyanna caught it.

'Wow, good catch,' said Mum.

'I would have caught it easily,' said Charlie.

Pollyanna went to put the milkshake back onto the shelf but the shelf was too high!' 'Wibble wobble,' said a little voice.

'Oh dear, are you cold?' Pollyanna asked the milkshake.

'No, I'm a milkshake aren't I? That's what we do, we shake and wobble.'

'Oh,' said Pollyanna and decided to put him in Mum's trolley.

'I saw that!' said Mum giving a little smile.

Pollyanna heard a lady ask her little boy to fetch her two tins of hot dogs. *Those dogs must be ever so tiny to fit into them tins, poor things, you'd think there would be some holes around the lid to cool them down a bit. How wicked!* Pollyanna thought.

It was the last aisle and Pollyanna looked over at the cream cakes. 'Umm,' she said, licking her lips as she looked at the chocolate brownies filled with delicious cream. 'Umm,' she said as she looked at the jam tarts, and then she noticed a pack of four cakes. 'Hot cross buns,' Pollyanna read. As she looked up in a daze there was a loud racket coming from the packet!

'Get over your side!' said a very cross bun.

'I am over my side!' said another very cross bun.

Suddenly they all started causing a racket inside of that packet. *'Enough!'* shouted Pollyanna.

'Pollyanna, come along silly, we're ready to pay now!' Dad called.

Pollyanna snapped out of her dream and ran to the checkout. Mum and Dad packed all the shopping.

As they were leaving the supermarket Charlie asked, 'What's for lunch then, Mum?'

And mum said, 'Toad in the hole.'

Pollyanna didn't feel very hungry at all ...

Baba

Kelly Shephard

One day Baba, the lamb, decided he would like to take a walk. 'Mummy, can I go for a walk up the mountain?'

'You need to ask your daddy. I don't want you walking up there alone, it's very dangerous and you do not know what strangers you will meet!'

Baba couldn't find his daddy anywhere, so he decided to walk up the mountains a little, not too far, so he could get back if his mummy called him. As he walked up the mountain he saw a little lamb in the distance. She was crying! Baba decided to walk up the mountain a little further.

'Are you okay?' There was no answer, so Baba decided to walk a little further. 'Excuse me, are you okay?'

The little lamb cried, 'No, please help me, I am trapped.'

Baba ran to rescue her. As he drew closer, he could see a fox snarling and watching them both! *'Arrrggggghhhhh!* What do you want?'

Baba replied, 'I heard the lamb crying, I just wanted to help!'

'Go away, you are not welcome, do you want to be trapped too?'

'No, Sir,' cried Baba. There was a huge bang and the nasty fox ran away.

'Oh thank you for coming to my rescue!' cried the little lamb.

'It's fine. I will try and set you free!' Baba pulled with all his strength to release the little lamb, but the harder he pulled, the more he became tangled.

'Please be careful, you mustn't get tangled as well!'

'What do you think you're doing?' growled the fox.

'I ... I tried to release the lamb!'

The horrid fox leapt towards them and tangled Baba up. 'That'll teach you!' the fox cackled.

'What are we going to do?' cried the lamb.

'Babaaaaa ... babaaaaa,' they both screamed, 'helpppp.'

Baba's daddy came rushing towards them and the fox scampered as fast as he could. 'Oh Daddy, I'm so sorry.'

'Baba, your mummy told you to come and find me. These mountains are very dangerous! You little lambs can't come up here without your parents. That fox may have eaten you both.' Baba's daddy freed them both and walked the little lamb back to her parents, who where very grateful and offered them tea and biscuits.

Baba never walked up the mountain alone ever again!

One Long Stormy Night

Stephanie Leese

It was one stormy night in Broughbery Forest, it was that stormy and scary it woke all of the animals in the forest. They made their way to a cave to see the boss of the forest, he was called Mr Gluster. He was a mean, old, grumpy gorilla who only liked his own company.

The animals made it to Mr Gluster's cave, and they started to shout in fear. Mr Gluster shouted, 'Be quiet, what a noise. We have gotten through a storm before, we can do it again, so shush, I need to think.'

Mr Gluster looked around his cave to see if anyone needed his help. 'Who needs my help, raise your hands and speak now,' said Mr Gluster miserably. He looked around the cave again and he could not see any hands raised, however he did hear a sound, not a very loud sound but a small voice coming from the back of the cave.

'Who was that?' shouted Mr Gluster, 'come forward and speak at once.'

Out popped a baby monkey and in a small voice he said, 'Please Mr Gluster help me find my mummy, she's lost and I'm hungry.'

Mr Gluster looked at the monkey called Snoops and said, 'Did your mummy come to my cave with you boy?'

'She told me to swing as fast as I could Sir and I did then I looked back and ... she was gone,' cried out Snoops.

The whole of the forest started to mutter amongst themselves, wondering what had happened to Snoops' mum, some of them started to talk loudly.

'Has she drowned Sir?'

'When monkeys get their fur wet they become heavy, she could have fallen off a tree,' tweeted a scared owl.

'Or struck by lightning,' shouted another.

Mr Gluster was getting very tired and annoyed with all of the forest animals. 'Will you be quiet, he is a baby, are you trying to scare him?' shouted Mr Gluster in an angry manner. Then he turned to Snoops, 'Snoops' mummy will be fine, we will look for her later, we are all tired and hungry, let's get some food and sleep, we will find your mummy, don't worry. There is honey in the rocks and water by the stones, help yourself everyone and get some rest,' yawned out Mr Gluster.

The forest animals went up one by one and helped themselves to the food and drink, then found a place to sleep.

Mr Gluster sat awake wondering what could have happened to Snoops' mum and thinking where she could be, he left it one hour and then woke some of the animals to help him search. First he woke Jaws the lion, he muttered, 'Can't a lion get some sleep?'

Then he woke up Chip the mole who yawned out, 'Is the storm over, are we going home?'

Mr Gluster whispered, 'No, I need your help to find the monkey's mum.'

They also woke up Rattles the rattlesnake and Kong the big mean ape. They all headed out into the storm to find Snoops' mum.

They walked, climbed, slithered and yelled, 'Droopy, Droopy,' but not a sound was heard.

Kong climbed the highest trees, Rattles slithered across forest floors, Mole dug underground but no sign of Droopy. They searched the forest for hours but had no sign of Snoops' mum anywhere. They headed back to the cave with sad faces, getting cold and wet every minute. They headed back in no hope of being able to find her, until they heard a yell not far from where they were.

'It's coming from the tree, Gluster,' Jaws roared out.

'OK, Kong I want you to be careful but climb the trees until you see her, be careful not to fall,' said Mr Gluster.

Kong climbed the trees and swung from branch to branch moaning about getting cold and wet, until he saw Snoops' mum. 'Hold on, I'm coming,' yelled Kong.

Kong reached Droopy, Snoops' mum and put her on his back, and climbed down to where Mr Gluster and the other brave animals were.

'Are you hurt?' asked Mr Gluster.

'No, but I am cold and so scared, where's my Snoops?' said Droopy, Snoops' mum.

'Snoops is fine, he's in my cave asleep, he is a very brave monkey.'

Knowing that her baby was OK the animals headed back to the cave avoiding the broken branches, lightning and the heavy rain.

They finally made it back to the cave wet, hungry and extremely tired but very pleased indeed. They'd found Snoops' mum and achieved making it back to the cave safe.

All of the other animals awoke to see Mr Gluster, Jaws, Chip, Kong, Rattles, and finally, Droopy, Snoops' mum back safe and secure.

Snoops ran up to his mum giving her the biggest hug in the world. 'I missed you Mummy,' said Snoops happily.

'I missed you too my baby,' said Droopy.

The animals all came together and they all gave out hugs and kisses to each other, because they were all happy that were all safe and sound in Mr Gluster's cave.

'Look, look,' shouted Snoops, 'it's morning and it's *sunny*.'

All of the animals were so happy that they had gotten through another storm without getting hurt, the clouds were white and the sky was blue, nothing could be better. They all thanked Mr Gluster one by one for making sure they were safe and for helping them get through another storm.

'You are all welcome in my cave every day, anytime. I am no longer grumpy and mean, I am Mr Gluster the kind gorilla who welcomes you all anytime.'

Mr Gluster had learnt a very big lesson that night and it was, treat people how you want to be treated, and from that day on Mr Gluster kept his word.

Twins

Susan Mullinger

Bethany, eight and a quarter was scared. It was nearly nine o'clock, a Monday morning, her first day at a new infants school. Three weeks ago she had moved to the northern town with her mother Joan. 'We are starting again,' her mother replied when Bethany had asked why they needed to move so far away from her old home. Several times at night, Bethany heard her mother arguing with her partner, Tom, but never thought they would have to leave him and their flat.

They moved into their new home during the Easter holidays and it had seemed a long wait for school to begin. 'It will give us time to explore our surroundings,' Mother said enthusiastically, 'we can go on picnics, make the most of the good weather.' Now, the dreaded day had arrived!

Tom and her mother in the end had not been able to hide their dislike for each other. Bethany accepted she would have to move and bravely tried not to show her mother how upset she felt. She could not get mother to understand why she was afraid of starting school. Bethany explained that since September children would have made friends, joined groups. She was going to be the odd one out. Being small for eight with red curly hair and millions of freckles was not going to help!

The teacher, Miss Walker, smiled encouragingly as Bethany walked hesitatingly into the classroom. The rest of the class gawped at the small girl with the large lunch box.

'Everybody say good morning to Bethany Giles, she is joining our class. Bethany, I was going to sit you next to Natalie but she's off sick. Do you think you will be alright by yourself until she returns?' Miss Walked asked.

She showed Bethany to a desk and explained, 'I'll be back when the rest of the class is settled.' Bethany was about to sit when her chair was pulled from under her and she landed on the floor. With reddening cheeks, Bethany, grabbed the plastic chair and sat. Behind her she could hear someone giggling and then begin chanting, 'Ha! Ha! Carrot top fell over.' Half turning she could see a huge boy laughing and the boy next to him was enjoying the joke.

Miss Walker heard the commotion, 'Tommy Jones and Nigel Green come here, don't dawdle. What do you think you are doing? We welcome new class members not make fun of them, apologise to

Bethany at once.' Tommy glared at Bethany as he returned to his place. She knew he was not finished with her.

Great, thought Bethany, *I have only been here an hour and already made one enemy. Playtime will be interesting.* She concentrated on the maths sheet she was given.

'Catherine, please could you show Bethany the way to the playground?' asked Miss Walker, 'help her find her way back to the classroom in twenty minutes.'

'Come on, hurry up slow coach,' said Catherine, 'my friends will be waiting for me, don't get into any trouble.' She left Bethany in the middle of the playground.

She tried to keep close to the playground assistant in the hope that Tommy would forget about her. If only they had not moved but remained in Tom's flat. Her mother moved effortlessly from place to place. Bethany could remember two previous moves when Mother had fallen out with her boyfriend. When they lived with Tom, Bethany hoped it was a permanent arrangement. She really missed him but tried not to show how upset she felt.

Recalling recent events, too late, Bethany realised she had wandered to the end of the playground. Tommy Jones and his mates were circling her. She had walked into a trap.

'Miss Perfect, curly hair, sweet and tiny - a real troublemaker boys. I can see I'll have to make her behave,' remarked Tommy, as he approached Bethany.

The sound of the whistle blowing long and loud broke the spell. Bethany ran back to the relative safety of her classroom with the words of Tommy ringing in her ears. *I wonder why that boy hates me so much* wondered Bethany turning her attention to her next lesson of literacy.

'Come and stand next to me Bethany,' said Miss Walker. 'Let me hear you read. Well done,' she exclaimed when Bethany reached the end of the page. 'You've obviously been taught well - you read with feeling.' Bethany remembered the hours spent with Tom, him reading to her and her reading to him. He always encouraged her and made reading enjoyable, she really did miss him!

At home time Bethany spotted Tommy Jones with his friends in the playground. She saw her mother standing in the opposite corner. Bethany sprinted diagonally across the area and ran straight into her mother's outstretched arms.

During the next nine days Tommy attempted to trip Bethany up at every opportunity. He was very threatening saying, 'I'll get you when you least expect it, mind your step or your turn will come carrot top.' Bethany dreaded going to school but did not tell her mother what was happening. She asked her mother to wait beside the main school door until she entered the building in the morning or to collect her when the day was over.

In lessons, Tommy continued to torment Bethany, often pulling her hair or throwing rubbers at her head. Generally he would try to distract her from her work. Tommy once accused Bethany of copying his answers in a test. Luckily, Miss Walker did not believe him.

Bethany decided that the best way to deal with Tommy was to ignore him. He could see she was no cry baby. Hopefully he would soon tire of his silly behaviour. It was not the first time since she had begun school that she was bullied. Bethany avoided contact with Tommy and his friends whenever possible.

One Monday morning Bethany was surprised to see another girl already sitting at her work desk. 'Hi, I'm Natalie, I've just had chickenpox, sorry I wasn't here when you arrived.'

In shock, Bethany stared open-mouthed at a girl who was smaller than her with even brighter red hair. Natalie said, 'You must have met my pain of a twin brother - pest of the classroom and unfortunately he sits behind us with Nigel Green.'

'Tommy Jones is your brother but he can't be, he's huge, fair haired, you're tiny like me.'

'I know,' replied Natalie, 'we are twins but not identical, that means we don't look alike,' she explained. 'I look like Mum and Tommy takes after Dad in looks and the way he behaves. He doesn't like me much, wishes he had a brother instead. Tommy had chickenpox when we were six. He acts the big guy here but at home he's a real softie.'

'I wish he would leave me alone,' Bethany sighed, 'he's been bullying me since we met.'

'Think I'd better have a chat with my dear brother at break,' said Natalie, as Miss Walker led the rest of the children, including a shuffling Tommy into the classroom.

Natalie kept her word and at break time told Tommy there was to be no more bullying. 'You will leave Bethany alone, we can't all be big like you, we all have different abilities. Like Mum says it is not difference that counts but having a kind heart which costs nothing.'

'Alright,' replied Tommy already moving away to another part of the playground.

'Is that it? Will Tommy stop bullying me?' asked Bethany.

'He'd better,' replied Natalie, 'or I'll remind him I'm the oldest. Mum says you should always listen to older people because they are often wiser than you. She also says violence never solves anything.'

'I think I like your mum,' said a smiling Bethany.

'Would you like to find out?' asked Natalie, taking a skipping rope out of her coat pocket, 'come for tea on Saturday, it will only be us because Tommy is going with Dad to football and they won't be back until late.'

After school Bethany told her mother all about her new friend and her invitation to tea.

The next morning she practically pulled her mother along the pavement to get to school as early as possible. 'See,' her mother was saying, 'I told you it would be alright.'

'Yes, Mum,' replied Bethany, noticing Natalie by the front door waving at her, 'bye Mum,' she called as she ran to her friend, 'bye.'

Clickety Click

Sheila O'Hara

'And that's the secret, Tom,' the old woman murmured ... 'and you must use it wisely.'

Tom hardly had time to ask her what she meant before she disappeared. She didn't walk or run away, she didn't go *poof* in a puff of smoke like some daft fairy in his sister's story book. She disappeared. Tom was nearly seven and he knew you couldn't just disappear because that wasn't possible. He sighed, had another biscuit and thought.

Tom liked thinking, especially thinking when he was eating biscuits. He found things out when he sat and thought. He repeated the riddle the old woman had given him.

'Clickety click, the lock it sticks
And the knob goes round and round.'

Well, thought Tom, *this is a to-do.* This was her secret and he had to use it wisely. *But I don't know anything about locks and doorknobs,* he thought, *if only I had a clue.* Tom had to leave the mystery as his mum called him for tea. 'It's fish fingers, Tom,' she called up the stairs. She always did that when it was fish fingers, because she knew these were magic words for Tom. 'Fish fingers, fish fingers, fish fingers,' you say it fast three times, spin around very quickly and stop! Then you make a wish. It always worked. Susan, Tom's big sister, said it worked because Tom always asked for chips to go with the fish fingers. Since Mum always put fish fingers and chips together, the wish was always granted.

'Ergo,' said sister, 'the idea of a wish is a total fallacy - there's no such thing as wishes, or wishes granted!'

Tom always nodded when Susan spoke, although he didn't agree with her. Of course there was wishes and magic. Anyway, Tom reasoned, Susan was speaking to some other boy. Who was Ergo anyway? Susan seemed to know him very well. 'Ergo, no fairies'! or 'Ergo, chips with fish'! To be honest, Tom didn't care for Ergo, he only seemed to be mentioned when Susan was being a particular know-it-all.

So, Tom ignored Susan, said fish fingers three times, spun round and sat down at the kitchen table.

'Clickety click, the lock that sticks
And the knob goes round and round,' came into his head.

'Well, I never,' said Tom, even though he didn't quite know it meant. But Gran always said it when she was surprised. He'd really meant to ask for chips, but here he was thinking about the old woman's gift, and that wasn't a way to get chips. Then a voice said, 'Look for the key!' It was all too confusing.

'He's gone again,' he heard Susan say, just as a chip bounced off his nose across the kitchen table.

'Stop that, Susan,' said Mum, 'Tom - stop daydreaming and eat up!'

'Do you have any spare keys, Mum?' asked Tom.

There was a silence and then, 'Spare keys? What for? Why do you want keys?'

Tom, who really didn't know why he'd asked the question, just ate his chips.

'There's a box of old keys in Grandpa's shed,' said Mum, 'but ask permission before you take any.'

Tom ran next door to his grandpa's house. Grandpa was in the garden and greeted Tom, 'Where's the fire young Tom?'

'Can I look at your keys please?'

'Keys?'

'Old box in the shed,' Tom gasped, 'can I look?'

'What kind of lock?'

'Clickety click,' started up in Tom's head and he cried, 'A sticky one!'

Grandpa laughed and led Tom into the shed, 'Here you are,' said Grandpa lifting Tom up onto a chair by the workbench, 'and here are the keys.' He turned as he walked out the shed, 'Enjoy yourself.'

Tom eyed the box of old keys and fell in love. He'd never seen such a treasure. They were all colours of gold and silver, there were red keys, and some yellow. And some had been painted green and blue and even purple, like Gran's hair.

He saw some very big keys like he'd seen in his pirate book and that one that opened the treasure chest. How had Grandpa got hold of that? Grandpa was a magician, so best not to ask. Hadn't he told Susan he'd make Susan disappear if she didn't stop tormenting Tom?

Now what, thought Tom. He didn't want to let the old woman down, but on the other hand ... he turned to his old standby and said fish fingers three times and clapped his hands. He's found that worked if he was ever scared in bed - obviously you couldn't spin round in bed - but he wasn't scared now, of course, well, not exactly. But well, he didn't really know about any of this.

'What do you want?' asked the Voice.

Tom nearly fell off the stool.

'What did you say?'

'I said, what do you want?' snapped the Voice and went on, 'Aren't you a big young to be deaf?'

'I'm not deaf,' said Tom, 'and you shouldn't be rude about ...'

'Well?'

'I can't see you,' said Tom.

'I'm not a show! You don't have to see me!' Then a giggle, 'Do you think it's television?' Obviously tickled by its own joke the Voice laughed out loud.

'Shush,' said Tom, 'Grandpa will hear you!'

'No he won't,' said the Voice, 'he really is d ...'

'Don't say it!' snapped Tom.

'Sorry, I'm sure.'

Tom just sat. Then the Voice said, 'Cat got your tongue?'

'I'm trying to work out what I want.'

'Well,' said the Voice, a touch sarcastically Tom thought, 'it might be something to do with keys, given that I am in charge of ... keys.'

'Clickety click the lock that sticks.'

'Who said that?' yelped the Voice.

'I suppose I did,' said Tom, 'do you know about the lock that sticks?'

'We all do - everyone in my line of work's been puzzling it for years.'

'I was told it by ...'

'Don't say her name, or she'll be back and we'll never get rid of her.'

'Oh dear,' sighed Tom, 'I'm all confused and just don't know ...'

'Look - none of these keys'll do it for you - I'll go and have a look and come back later.'

Tom just nodded and the Voice went quiet.

Grandpa came into the shed, 'How're you going with the keys?'

'Not well,' said Tom, 'not well at all, but I expect help quite soon.'

Grandpa laughed, 'Tom, you sound like you have the weight of the world on you.'

'Not the world Grandpa - just a door.'

'What do you mean?'

'Clickety click, the lock that sticks,' said Tom.

'Your gran teach you that?'

'No,' said Tom, 'it was ...'

'No matter,' said Grandpa, 'I must press on - but remember ice cream at six o'clock in the garden.'

Tom nodded and as Grandpa left he picked up a huge key, exactly like the key to the door to the tunnel in Wonderland and tried fitting it into Grandpa's collection of old locks.

'That one fits,' he shouted.

'Of course it does,' said the Voice, 'I've just brought it!'

'You're back,' said Tom.

'You're welcome,' said the Voice.

'Clickety click ...' began Tom, and turned the key, then shouted, 'the lock doesn't stick!' He jumped off the chair and ran around shouting, 'I've found it, I've found it.'

'You're welcome!' said the Voice again.

'Now what?' said Tom, 'what about the knob that goes round and round?'

'Don't do knobs,' said the Voice, 'I'm a key man, me.'

Voice went silent.

Tom had one of his grandpa's biscuits and thought he'd sorted the riddle. He had the key which fitted the lock which didn't stick, if he could find the knob he would know the secret.

And then he forgot all about it.

He settled into Grandpa's old armchair and thought some more. It was all nothing of matter anyway, who cared about the wise old woman, and secrets and magic. But Grandpa had her key so, reasoned Tom, Grandpa was magic and he cared about Grandpa. Ergo, as Susan would say, Tom cared about magic.

Tom closed his eyes the better to think, and woke up to see the doorknob in the shed door go round and round. He heard voices from outside.

'He's locked himself in,' said Susan.

'He's fallen asleep,' said Grandpa.

'Maybe he's fallen and hurt his head,' cried his mum.

Tom's eyes could hardly stay open, he was so tired.

'Try the key, Tom,' said Gran, 'like I told you.'

Tom heard the wise old woman's voice again, just like when he was falling asleep last time Gran babysat for him (though Tom knew he wasn't a baby). He could hear the nursery rhyme all about clocks and locks, something about tickety-tock goes the clock as it hung upon the wall, then clickety click the lock. Tom realised who the old woman was.

'The knob on the door ...' started Tom.

'Don't try the knob ...' said Gran, 'you must turn the key, Tom, just turn the key.

'There's ice cream!' piped up Mum.

'Listen Tom,' said Susan, 'just listen!'

There was some whispering outside the door, and then.

'Fish fingers, fish fingers, fish fingers!' cried the whole family and then *clap! Clap! Clap!*

Tom grabbed Alice's key and put it in the lock, he grasped the doorknob firmly and said, 'The doorknob will *not* go round and round,' and, just like magic, the key turned and the door opened.

Tom rather liked the fuss, especially the double helping of ice cream.

'I'm glad you used the secret wisely, Tom,' said Gran as she was putting him to bed later.

'Thank you Gran,' said Tom, 'I'll keep it safe.'

Tom smiled as he snuggled down to sleep, Gran need never know that he hadn't any idea what she was talking about.

The Hungry Dragon Goes To Besco

Nanny H

It was a hot summer's day. Miles had been excused from school early because he had to pay a visit to Mrs Bobbins his dentist, for a check up, at least that is what his mother had told him.

He was a little nervous about going because it was the first time he had been for a check up. His dad had told him not to worry, that Mrs Bobbins would only look into his mouth and if he had been cleaning his teeth every day, she would be pleased with him and give him a *good boy* badge to stick on his jumper.

After his dad had told him this he didn't feel so bad. After all, his cousins Rachael and Nicola had been for check ups at the dentist, and they always came home happy and smiling and not only did they have *good girl* badges they had been given a present off their mum for behaving well.

So off Miles went feeling quite grown up, walking by the side of his mum, who was pushing his baby sister, Amelia, in her pram, thinking to himself, *if I behave well maybe Mum will buy me a present too, perhaps a new toy or something just like my cousins,* and this is what his mother did.

She took him to a toyshop in town and told him to choose himself something out of the toys displayed in the window, but she did mention that it wasn't to be too expensive.

He stood and gazed at all the lovely toys. There was such an assortment it was hard for him to decide what to choose.

Should I have the car on the shelf with the red roof, he thought, *or maybe the ninja Action Man figure that was hanging from a rope.* There was a cute teddy in a red skirt his sister Amelia would like and a brightly coloured green and blue striped ball his cousin Jordan would like too.

His cousin Jordan was at the crawling stage and loved playing on the floor rolling a ball back and forth with his dad, but never mind them, he was the one who had been to the dentist. His sister Amelia only had gums and Jordan's teeth were all brand new, so there was no need for them to go to the dentist yet.

After a while of looking around the shop window, the toy that caught his eye the most was the figure of the green dragon with the red ears and the big blue spikes protruding from his back.

He stared and stared at the dragon because it was so lifelike, it looked so sad, it even looked as if it had been crying, in fact he thought he saw it move. All of a sudden he felt quite warm just like someone had lit a bonfire behind him. He turned around and there, right in front of him, stood the exact image of the dragon that he had been looking at in the shop window, but this time it didn't just look lifelike it was alive and it was about eight feet tall.

Miles just stood there, he felt so small as he looked up to this green monster. His body was shaking all over and although he tried to lift his legs and run, he was fixed to the spot, he just couldn't move. He tried to scream but not a sound would come out of his mouth, not even a whimper.

The dragon looked down at Miles and opened his mouth. Thoughts of fear raced through the little boy's head. He had watched a television programme the week before and he knew all about dragons and how they blew fire out of their mouths, but instead of this happening all that came out of this dragon's mouth was a load of hot air, and garbled (mixed up talk) as if the dragon was trying to say something.

At first Miles was puzzled, then all of a sudden he had a strange ringing noise in his ears and for some unknown reason he could understand every word the dragon said.

'Don't be afraid,' said the dragon, 'I am not going to hurt you, I just want you to tell me where I can get some dragon food, I have been sitting in that shop window for so long I am starving.'

Miles stood there feeling very confused. How could this be happening and how could he understand dragon language? Should he answer the dragon? After all he had always been told not to talk to strangers, but the dragon looked so sad and thin from hunger that Miles decided that if he only told the dragon where he could buy dragon food and not go with him it couldn't do any harm.

'Well,' said Miles still shaking in his shoes, 'I don't know really where to get dragon food but there is a pet shop up the top of town called Little Butties Pet Shop where they might sell dragon food.'

So off up the town went the green dragon towards the pet shop. Nobody else in the town seemed to be able to hear or see the dragon, only Miles.

The dragon went into the pet shop, although he had to lower his head because he was so tall, and leave his tail trailing outside the shop door, he just about managed to see what was in the shop window, but all he could see was cat, dog and fish food, but no dragon food.

The green dragon was really annoyed and getting hungrier by the minute. He stomped out of the pet shop shouting, 'Food, give me food, I am starving,' looking for the little boy who had sent him on a wasted journey to a shop that didn't sell dragon food. No one else could see or hear the dragon only Miles who could hear the noise the dragon was making as far away as the toyshop that he was looking in for his present with his mum.

What could he do to calm the dragon down? Suddenly he had a good idea. I could tell the dragon they sell dragon food in Woolies Store, after all they sell almost everything else in there. So into Woolies the dragon went, and while he was inside the store Miles hid behind red post box just in case the dragon couldn't find dragon food once again.

After a while of hiding and peeping from behind the post box feeling rather frightened, Miles heard a mighty roar. He could see the dragon coming out of Woolies store blowing smoke and fire and in a terrible rage shouting once again, 'Food, give me food, I am starving.'

'Oh dear,' Miles said to himself, 'I don't think they sell dragon food in there either, what am I going to do now?' Miles decided the best thing to do now, was to make a run for it back to the toyshop where he had left his mother.

The dragon by this time had made his way to the post box where Miles was hiding and because the dragon was so tall he could see Miles running away. He chased after Miles who had run into a side street. It didn't seem like any normal side street, all the houses were painted in bright colours and all the doorknobs were all the same bright-red, it looked just like something out of a fairy tale story.

Miles ran and ran not quite sure where the street would take him. All he knew was that if he did not think of something fast to get rid of this raging dragon he was in trouble.

If only he could find the supermarket that his mum did her shopping in. They sold everything you could ever think of from a toothbrush to a colour television and every type of food possible. His mother always got everything she needed there.

Miles ran as fast as his legs could take him with the dragon following. For some unknown reason he could run much faster than he normally did, he felt really strange. The red knobs on the doors seemed to whiz by at high speed. All of a sudden as if by magic, at the end of the brightly coloured street appeared sparkling in the bright sunshine the most beautiful coloured superstore you have ever seen.

It had a huge sign in front of it; *Besco store welcomes everyone and sells everything:* Did this mean it welcomed dragons and sold dragon food.

How could this happen? thought Miles, it usually takes at least a twenty minute journey by the Besco free bus to get here and I have got here in no time.

The green dragon had caught up with Miles, he was a lot calmer and the fire and smoke had stopped coming out of his mouth but he was still shouting, 'Food, give me food, I'm starving.' The Besco store looked so inviting that Miles sent the dragon in there, hoping from the bottom of his heart that the dragon could find what he wanted in there to satisfy his hunger.

Being such a big store the dragon found it a little difficult to find the pet food aisle. There was plenty of helpful staff around but because they couldn't hear or see him, he couldn't ask them the way. At last he found the aisle where they sold pet food but again there was no dragon food.

But wait, what was that smell? Was it dragon food? It smelt delicious so the green dragon made his way to where the smell was coming from. He couldn't believe his eyes. He saw in front of him lots of hungry people tucking into food, delicious food.

What was it? he thought. *Should I try it?* Why not, everyone else seemed to be enjoying it. Well because he was a dragon and he could blow fire out of his mouth the skin around his lips was thick and he could pick up hot things without feeling pain, so he made his way to the meal counter and helped himself to the complete tray of pie and chips.

The chairs in the restaurant were too small for the dragon, so he sat on the floor and leant against a wall. He tucked into the meal as if he had never eaten before. He felt so happy and contented he just lay there, saying to himself, 'Full at last, what a great meal.'

He remembered the little boy who had helped him to find food and felt a little ashamed that he had treated him so badly, but he knew he had only raged because he wanted food because he was starving.

The dragon was feeling tired after all the food he had eaten, so he thought that if he made his way back to the toyshop window for a sleep, maybe just maybe the little boy might still be there, making his mind up which toy to choose.

'Miles,' said his mum, 'come on haven't you made your mind up yet? You are not daydreaming again are you? We are supposed to be going to Besco for dinner.'

'Yes Mum,' said Miles looking at the toy dragon in the shop window, who seemed to look a little fatter, 'can I have the green dragon, the one with the smiley face and can I have some dragon food for dinner? Er, I mean pie and chips.'

Untitled

ASW

Once upon a time on a bright and sunny day, there stood a tall and elegant ash tree, in a woodland far away.

A young man came walking by, looking at the tree, he said, 'Hello Mr Ash would you mind terribly if I were to take one of your new shoots to plant into my garden in my new house?' Knowing the tree would not answer, he began to take up ever so gently a small young shoot and placing it into a large pot carried it to his car. As he was about to drive away he looked back at the ash tree and said thank you, with a smile on his face.

On arriving at his home he took the tree into his garden and planted it near to his fence making sure it was well planted and tied it to a strong stake for protection from the wind. He then stood back to admire what he knew was to be, then smiling to himself he went indoors. The young man had a son whose name was Adam. Now he was just old enough to play in the garden, so his father picked him up and took him to the window to show him the tree he had just planted and said, 'One day Adam it will be tall and strong just as you will be.'

Summer was fast approaching, and as Adam looked out of the window he saw that the tree was filling up with leaves facing up to the bright sunshine, but as yet not very tall.

Adam asked his mother if he could go out and play in the garden. 'Yes,' she replied, so he picked up his ball and went outside, he was gaily bouncing his ball along the path when he heard someone call to him, he was startled as he knew he should be alone. 'Who's there?' he whispered.

'It is I,' came the reply.

At first Adam felt afraid, as he could see nobody at all.

Ash again spoke saying, 'Look at the tree it is me talking to you.'

'But trees cannot talk,' said Adam.

'Oh but I can,' said the tree, 'and my name is Ash, and what do they call you young man?'

Adam told the tree his name.

'Well hello Adam,' said Ash.

'Hello,' was Adam's hesitant reply.

'Can you really talk?' asked Adam.

'Yes,' said Ash, 'but we must keep this our little secret and will you be my friend?'

'Yes of course,' replied Adam.

Adam sat down by Ash and they started to talk to one another, they seemed to be talking for ages, when Adam heard a voice saying, 'Who are you talking to Adam?' It was his mother.

'Oh! Um! To Ash, Mummy,' but Ash stayed silent.

'Oh! I see,' said his mother looking bemused, 'well your lunch is ready so you have to come in now.'

Adam stood up, looked at Ash, waved and went indoors for his lunch.

Adam washed his hands and went into the kitchen, his father was at the table, and he looked at his father and smiled a knowing smile.

When his mother had placed his meal on the table and sat down she turned to his father and said, 'Adam was sitting on the ground talking to that tree you planted last year. You will have to talk to him and tell him not to be so silly, talking to a tree indeed.'

After Adam had finished his lunch his father turned to him and said, 'Now what is all this about talking to a tree?'

Adam explained about his friend Ash, his father looked at him, raised his eyebrows, smiled and said, 'Everyone needs a friend in life.'

'Yes Daddy,' he replied.

Now Adam could not wait to go back out into the garden again and talk to Ash, so he asked his mother if he could once again go out to play in the garden. 'Very well,' said his mother, 'but no talking to that silly tree again.'

Adam rushed out and went straight to Ash, 'Hello Ash,' said Adam.

'Hello,' said Ash, 'and what did you have for your lunch today?'

'Food to make me grow tall and strong.'

'Oh!' said Ash, 'I use the sun, the rain and a long winter sleep to help me to grow tall, but how tall will I be?' said Ash.

Adam looked at Ash and said, 'Well, you will be a lot taller than me because all trees grow very tall, soon you will be tall enough to see over our fence to the world outside!'

'Oh! And will you Adam?'

'No, that will never be,' said Adam.

Ash became very excited as Adam told him of the great height he would one day become.

The two of them would talk and talk right through the summer, and as autumn approached, Ash began to tell Adam that soon he would have to go to sleep for the winter. 'Why?' asked Adam.

'Because I must,' said Ash, 'and as soon as all my lovely leaves have dropped away, I will sleep until the next spring.'

'I will miss you,' said Adam.

'And I you,' said Ash.

Autumn arrived and all the leaves had fallen from Ash, he said goodnight to Adam, 'See you in the spring.' Adam felt sad at not being able to talk to his friend for so long, and every day he would look out of the window waiting for spring to arrive.

Then one morning Adam saw out of the window that Ash was waking up to the springtime.

The sun was shining very brightly this day so Adam asked his mother if he could go out to play in the garden. 'Of course you can,' she replied.

Well, when Adam opened the door he could hear Ash shouting with excitement, 'Oh do come here,' said Ash.

'What is it?' said Adam.

'Oh, I can now see over the fence, and you were right, I have grown taller, I can see all the other trees around. Oh what a lovely sight, green fields, flowers and oh look, a rabbit playing in the field, how wonderful it all is, and I will be able to see it always.'

Adam was standing very quiet.

What is wrong?' said Ash.

'Well,' said Adam, 'I will never be tall enough to see over the fence.'

'Oh!' said Ash, 'I see, well why not climb up to the top of my branches, then you will see all that I can see.'

'What a good idea,' said Adam, 'but is it safe?'

'I will help you,' said Ash.

'So up he climbed to the very top holding tightly to Ash.

'How lovely it all is,' said Adam excitedly, 'how lucky you are.'

'Well now you can share all of this with me,' said Ash, 'you will be able to climb up here every day from now on while I am awake.'

It seemed ages that they had been talking and admiring the view, when Adam heard a loud voice calling for him to get down at once, it was his mother and she sounded furious. Adam climbed down to his mother, and she said, 'If I see you up that tree again I will not let you out to play again.' Adam knew that his mother meant what she said by the tone of her voice, so he promised not to climb again. 'See that you keep your promise,' she said before going indoors.

'Well, what are we going to do now?' said Adam.

'Not to worry,' said Ash, 'I will tell you everything I see every day, it will be like telling you a story.'

'That would be wonderful,' said Adam, so he sat down close to Ash while he told him all that was happening over the fence. Adam sat for hours every day listening with a happy smile.

Summers and winters seemed to approach more quickly as the years passed by and Adam came out to see his friend less and less as he grew older, but he never forgot his old friend completely.

Then one day when he was out seeing Ash for what he thought may be the last time, he slowly walked up to his old friend, stood for what seemed a very long time just looking at Ash, then he said, 'Hello old friend.'

'Hello Adam, what's wrong?'

Adam began to explain that he was about to get married and leave home and today was his wedding day. 'I will miss you old friend.'

'I am sure you will come to see me from time to time,' said Ash.

'I will,' said Adam, 'and I will never forget you, I promise.'

Adam seemed lost for words, Ash could sense this so he said, 'Adam there is one thing you could do for me before you leave.'

'Anything,' said Adam.

'Well you could take one of my new shoots as your father did all those years ago, then plant it in your garden to grow with your children and to be their friend.'

'What a great idea,' said Adam, 'and as you will be able to see my new garden I will plant it near to my fence so that you will see it growing as tall as you, knowing the friendship we shared will be there forever giving my children a friend.'

Adam did as Ash had requested and took a nice young shoot and put it gently into a large pot ready to be planted in his own garden. Adam touched the trunk of Ash tenderly and said, 'Goodbye for now my very dear friend.'

'Goodbye,' said Ash, 'and come and see me when you can.'

'I will,' said Adam, then he turned and walked indoors.

The first opportunity Adam had he planted his young shoot as close to the fence as he could, making sure it was firmly planted as his father had done, stood back, smiling knowingly. Then he realised that when he was a young boy and his mother had asked his father to talk to him about Ash, his father had smiled in the same way.

Pamela Goes To Craigmount

Caroline Anne Carson

It was awful. It was Pamela Watson's first day at Craigmount which was a boarding house for girls who attended Craighill School. She sat scowling on the edge of her bed whilst other members of her dormitory rifled through her suitcase, tossing things in the air, laughing and making rude comments. Pam had packed things herself because she had had no one to help her. Her father had left, her mother was ill and her grandmother had died suddenly. Pam was just twelve years old and her younger brother, Tom, aged seven-and-a-half was sent to live with an aunt.

Pam finally got really angry with a girl, called Annie Carter, who was waving a pair of Pam's knickers around. Pam's fist shot out and caught Annie on the nose. Blood spurted everywhere and there was a sudden hush. *Click, click, click* was heard outside the dormitory as the housemistress, Mrs Turner, marched in high heels towards the new girls' dormitory. The door swung open and Mrs Turner gasped when she saw Annie and the blood on her face. 'What happened to you Annie?' Mrs Turner demanded.

'I hit my head on the wall,' squeaked Annie.

Pam jumped up, 'No she didn't, Mrs Turner, I punched her.'

'Annie, go to Matron straightaway. Pamela, come with me.'

Pam, trembling, followed Mrs Turner out of the dormitory and into Mrs Turner's office.

Mrs Turner was firm but kind and she let Pam explain what had happened. Pam was given a punishment of having to help with the washing-up for a week. Mrs Turner told her to apologise to Annie and finish putting away her things as quickly as possible before lunch.

Matron had quickly helped Annie's nose to stop bleeding and Annie had returned to the dormitory when Pam returned from Mrs Turner's office. 'Sorry I hit you, Annie,' said Pam.

Annie shrugged her shoulders and said, 'I shouldn't have been teasing you about your clothes.'

'Oh well,' said Pam, 'can we be friends.'

'We sure can!' said Annie, 'come on let's go down to the dining room for lunch.'

In the dining room they queued up for their lunch which was sausage rolls, chips and salad with banana custard for pudding. Pam and Annie sat at a table with four other girls from their dormitory - Jane Hume, Elizabeth (Liz) Fenton, Joanne Hawke and Joanna (Jo) Beadle.

It was strange, that first night, getting into bed amongst five other beds. The girls were all friends now and they whispered to each other about their first day but not for long as they quickly fell asleep.

In the morning the new girls were surprised by the rising bell which was rung vigorously by Mrs Turner. None of them got out of bed until Mrs Turner flung the dormitory door open and snapped, 'Up you get girls. Hurry along and get washed at the toilet area. You've got fifteen minutes before breakfast.'

The girls tumbled out of bed, grabbed their wash bags and queued for the basins and toilets. It was a mad rush to get washed, dressed in the school uniform which included a tie, get their beds nearly aired and be down to breakfast in quarter of an hour. They managed in time and ate a hearty breakfast. Pam had to race up to the dormitory to make her bed and tidy her things ahead of the others because she had to help the kitchen staff with the dishes. She worked in the kitchen until the bell rang which signalled it was time to leave the boarding house and walk to school. She was glad to go and meet her friends but the kitchen staff were very kind to her and gave her some biscuits for morning tea.

At lunchtime the boarders returned to the boarding house for lunch and went back to school in time for the afternoon lessons. It was at lunchtime that any mail was handed out. Pam longed to get a letter but she didn't receive one for the whole of the first term.

All the boarders had two bath nights a week each and on the other days they had to wash at the basins. They could wash their hair whenever they wished but it was new girls' job to wash the brushes and combs on a Thursday lunchtime and lay them out on top of a cupboard on the landing to dry on towels. Pam had thick dark brown shoulder length hair which she wore in bunches with a thick fringe. Annie had honey-blonde wavy chin-length hair, Liz had hair like Pam's but she wore it in plaits, Jo had short curly red hair and Joanne had straight platinum blonde hair which she wore in a ponytail without a fringe.

The new girls settled into life at Craigmount very well. Pam was surprised that she was voted head of the dormitory. It was her responsibility to make sure everyone was in bed before Mrs Turner put the lights out at 8.30pm. She also had to organise a roster for cleaning the dormitory and see that it was done.

A week before the end of Pam's first term at Craigmount there was an exciting announcement made by Mrs Turner at breakfast. There was going to be a dance for all the boarders, from the twelve-year-olds to the sixth formers, with the boys from the neighbouring boarding house, Gladstone. Pam and her friends were thrilled. It was going to be on the last Saturday of the term. Parents and guardians had been asked to allow money for new dresses up to a specified amount - the girls went in groups to buy their new dresses. Pam, Liz, Jo, Annie and Joanne went with matron to town after school on the Tuesday. After much hesitation all of them purchased a new dress. They were not ball dresses, just simple but modern and attractive outfits. When the day of their dance arrived there were photographs taken of each dormitory group dressed for the dance. It was held in Gladstone in the large dining room and there were refreshments served at the end. All the girls enjoyed themselves.

On the last evening of term, Mrs Turner gave out certificates and awards. A girl called Mary from another dormitory got the most untidiness marks that had ever been known at Craigmount so her dormitory did not win the award for being the tidiest! Pam's dormitory did not win it either. However her dormitory got a special mention for being clean. After the awards there was a singsong and the kitchen staff dished out buttered toast and cocoa drinks. Pam was quite sad that the term had ended, but her mother was better, she heard from Mrs Turner, so she could go home for the holidays.

What A Wonderful Book

Gloria Thorne

All the books on the bookshelf were nudging each other, and being mean to the dictionary. They said he was fat, they said he was dull, and they said he was old and smelly. They all made his life very unhappy.

The other books were brightly coloured and full of interesting stories of adventure, wild animals, sea monsters and magicians There were also puzzle books and colouring books. The children, Olivia and Emma, loved them, but they never went near the dictionary, who sat huddled, neglected and miserable. He didn't have a single friend on the bookshelf, and no one even bothered to dust him.

Most of the books had been given to the children by their family and friends, but the dictionary had been found in the attic many years ago, and just plonked on the bookshelf.

He was fat because he was full of so many colourful words from which you could make up lots of brilliant stories. And he only looked dull because his jacket was made of black leather; but this was far grander than any of the other book-jackets, especially the paperbacks, which had become torn and creased, particularly the favourites. He'd heard it said that he'd last for years yet, whereas the children would eventually grow out of the other books and send them off to charity shops and car-boot sales.

One evening when Olivia and Emma had gone to bed, the books decided they didn't want the dictionary to sit with them a minute longer. The puzzle book, who was by far the brightest, had a good idea. 'Say you guys, if we all push and heave together, we could push the boring old dictionary off the shelf and then there'd be more room for us.'

But the dictionary wasn't going to let them get rid of him without putting up a fight. He was, after all, older and wiser than they were, and he still had a little pride left. And so the more the books pushed, the more he sat firm. But in the end they were too strong for him, and with a great thud, he fell to the floor. He screamed with pain as he landed on his spine, and sobbed bitterly when he felt some of his pages crumple.

All night he lay there until Olivia came looking for him next morning. He was so amazed that anyone should actually bother to look for him that he held his breath and nearly choked.

Olivia had written a lovely story which she was entering for a school prize, but there were one or two words she wasn't sure how to spell -

and spelling was very important at her school. She was so pleased when she found them in the dictionary, after her mother had shown her how to look them up. Then she gently put him back on the shelf, after trying to get the creases out of pages. She put him next to one of her colouring books, who rudely ignored him.

Next day Olivia arrived home from school thrilled. She'd won a prize for her story, and the teacher had said how good her spelling was. She told her mother what a great help the dictionary had been, and gave him an affectionate pat. Oh dear, this made him cry out in pain, as his poor spine was still bruised and sore.

But after this, the dictionary's life changed completely. He was still fat, of course, but Olivia had tenderly polished his leather jacket until it shone. He felt as proud as could be.

Then the other books felt very ashamed of themselves, and they all apologised to him for their unkind behaviour. They all wanted to be his friend now, and gave him pride of place on the bookshelf. The dictionary had never been so happy.

The Velvet Unicorn

Yolanda Lindsay Mabuto

A small castle lay deep in the forest, where the army fairies hovered the corridors at night and the soldier butterflies during the day. The air smelt of white roses as the sky shimmered like a crimson sea scattered with golden pebbles.

Loud cheers echoed along the castle walls, as people gathered to witness the celebration of the birth of the forest princess. A small baby girl bundled in purple cloth lay in the arms of her mother. 'I pronounce my daughter Violete,' announced Lord Mauve, kissing the queen on her cheek. 'She will grow up to be the purple blossom of this family, not only will she represent beauty and grace but also good judgement.'

The first queen was jealous, as she had been unable to give the king a child. The two queens who housed this castle were named after the most rare and beautiful colour of the flowers in the forest. Colour of royalty, Queen Velve and Queen Viole. The king himself had been named King Mauve after his great grandfather, who believed in the mystery of purple and its power in preserving excitement, fantasy and joy.

After the king praised Violete he said, 'Although Velve has been unable to bless me with an heir she still remains dear to me and I hope she will accept Violete as her own.'

Forcing a smile, Queen Velve nodded and replied, 'I already love her as my own.' Although she seemed to bear love for the girl, all she could think of was how to get rid of her. Jealousy and anger filled her heart. The ceremony was to start immediately after the gifts had been presented. The ritual was that each king would complete the circle of life by placing a precious stone in the circle of the baby's life. At a certain age she'd be able to open the circle and be given her freedom. The gifts were to be given by the four kings of the neighbouring forests. King Rouge gave a ruby, followed by King Sable with a bright sapphire, and then King Gale, a shimmering topaz, then King Groene gave her a stunning emerald. Lastly her father placed the biggest purple gem to complete the ring of his daughter's circle of life, tied with grace and beauty and honour to the five forests.

After the ceremony, Queen Velve left the castle and ran to the deepest part of the forest. Her eyes were streaming with tears as she sat by a quiet river. Her pain made her heart ache heavily. As her last tear dropped into the water, 'Why do you cry?' she heard. 'Why are you hurting?' the voice added.

'Who are you?' asked Velve.

'I am Sade, the river's fairy-angel of sadness,' she replied.

'I have been unable to give Mauve an heir for twelve years, and his second wife within a short time has given him a beautiful daughter,' she sulked. 'I wish it could have been me and not her,' she cried.

Sade was a river fairy-angel who only granted wishes that cause harm to others by merely displacing sorrow from one person to another. 'I can help you,' she whispered, as she handed Velve a bluebell and a pearl. 'Bluebells are in the same family as hyacinths. The classical hyacinth was a flower described to have sprung from the blood of a dying prince. This bluebell will bring upon Violete the same death. As each petal falls, her death nears. The pearl represents Violete's circle of life. Once you put the pearl in the bluebell, the curse will begin to surround her just as the petals surround the pearl. When the pearl darkens, death would have arrived,' she explained. 'But I must warn you, only the rarest creature can save her.'

Queen Velve was not sure if she wanted to kill Violete. Tears filled her eyes but her pity for Violete was overpowered by her bitterness.

'Hurry along and beware of the rarest creatures,' Sade said as she slowly returned back into the water.

'Wait!' cried Velve, but she was too late, the fairy-angel had disappeared. She dried her tears and walked back to the castle.

That night, Velve could not sleep. Instead she sat up all night watching the stars..

'Velve,' a soft voice said, shaking her. 'Velve, why are you asleep by the window?' Viole asked. Velve jumped off quickly as her heart sank.

'Here's your breakfast,' Voile said as she left the room. Viole had always treated her like her mother.

'The only heir that Mauve should have should be from me, even if it takes a thousand more years,' she uttered. 'Guards!' yelled Velve. Immediately four yellow gnome guards were standing in front of her. 'Search the forest for the rarest creatures and bring them to me.'

'What, your Majesty?' asked one gnome.

'What right do you have to question me?' she roared back.

Terrified, the guards ran out.

After a busy day, night returned. 'You found what?' Velve screamed.

'We are not sure,' one replied.

'What?' she bellowed. 'Where is it?' she yelled, smashing a vase to the floor as she struck the table.

'Ah ah ...' stuttered the shortest gnome. 'It disappeared,' the gnome replied.

'You helpless ...'

'What's going on in here?' interrupted King Mauve.

Shaken by the king's unannounced appearance, Velve thought of a quick lie as the gnomes bowed frantically.

'Stop bowing!' groaned Mauve. 'Why are you not outside with the other guards?'

'I called them,' Velve stuttered. 'I heard something outside my window.'

Mauve was not convinced as he looked at the broken vase and stared at the guilty faces of the gnome guards. 'Guards, get back outside and check whatever is outside her window, he murmured. He left the room and the guards followed.

'He will never know,' she reassured herself. She sat on her bed and mumbled, 'A velvet unicorn, that's impossible. It must be killed before it frees Violete from the curse.

Next day, Velve went to the river to look for Sade. 'Sade, where are you? There might be a rare creature in the forest,' she whispered, hoping Sade would appear. After a while she gave up and returned to the castle.

Night to day. Day to night. Years passed and finally a couple of petals had fallen. 'At last,' she sighed. She hurried down the corridor to look at Violete. She lay silent in her crib, so peacefully. *Death awaits you,* Velve thought as she stroked Violete's dark hair.

'Isn't she gorgeous,' Viole announced, startling Velve.

'You frightened me.'

Viole and Velve talked through the night until they both fell asleep in the baby's room.

Viole's eyes flickered open. 'What a lovely morning,' she yawned, waking up Velve. Walking to wards the crib, 'Argh!' she screamed.

'What is it?' yelled Viole, joining her at the crib. There was no one in it.

'Mauve, get up! Violete has disappeared,' screeched Viole.

While Viole told Mauve, Velve went to check the bluebell. All the petals had fallen and the pearl had turned lilac.

'What?' Mauve howled as he got up from bed in haste.

After a thorough search the king called his men. Soldiers flocked to search for Violete.

Meanwhile in the same castle, beneath it lay the princess. She had not died and had become invisible to the people in the castle.

The search for Violete was endless. Many years had passed and after mourning Violete for so long, the misery made Viole become ill. Velve nursed her guilt; she knew she would never tell anyone what she had done.

Beneath the castle, Violete was growing into a beautiful girl. Hazel eyes, dark hair and earthly skin. An old woman mothered her, from the very day she had vanished from the castle. A woman who had died because of trying to protect her family. The time had come for the truth to be known.

Velve was the only heir of a great chain of Nacre sorcerers. After refusing to take over the powers of her father's chain, her mother had to sacrifice her life in exchange for Velve's freedom and allow the father to re-marry and have another first heir. On her deathbed, her mother wished her to be childless, this would be the only way she would be able to return and keep her powers in her grave and revenge the new wife and heir. The new wife was me and the heir was Viole,' she said sadly. 'After realising this I gave my life to the bluebirds, the ultimate quincunx of life. My death would be short if my daughter had a daughter. Her strength would help me fight Velve and her mother for good. Echo, Shadow, Nightmare, Whisper and Shimmers, the five bluebird spirits that form the quincunx key to the gift of enchantment gave me the power I need to destroy all curses. They unlock the mysterious fierce power of the violet stone that is known to be the heart of the velvet unicorn. The unicorn that serves as the guardian of the night forest. The velvet unicorn is the last hope for destroying any curse.'

Mauve never stopped his search. Then one day he found a book which he read, 'The bluebirds unleash the truth of any curses.' He immediately ordered the gnome guards to leave the castle and find these birds. Mauve was convinced that his castle had been cursed.

After many miles, the gnome guards found the five beautiful birds. The quincunx, Echo, Shadow, Nightmare, Whisper and Shimmers. 'We know you are looking for us, and the time has come for the forest to be at peace,' they sang. 'We will guide you in spirit.'

The guards hurried back to the castle and told Mauve what the birds had said. 'At sunset, follow the flame lilies.'

Sunset came and the gnome guards and Mauve left the castle without letting Velve or Viole know. The paths were endless, then finally they could hear the crashes of water. They followed this sound. A fountain stood there. There by the shimmering fountain stood the most beautiful mare any forest creature had ever seen. Its mane glowed in the remaining rays of the sunset and its horn was a perfect white. The velvet unicorn. A gnome guard whispered, 'Bluebird spirits, cast your powers now.'

The quincunx shuffled into place, Echo, Shadow, Nightmare and Whispers at the corners and Shimmers in the centre. As they came into position, streams of glowing glitter flowed out of their feathers and combined to form a dark purple stone. The stone slowly descended and drifted towards the unicorn. As the unicorn drank from the fountain the stone pierced its chest with a massive explosion. The unicorn's coat deepened to a saddened velvet. A ray of white light trailed from its tail, as it galloped in rage back and forth.

'What now?' asked the gnome guard.

'We wait,' replied Shimmers. Shimmers was the wisest and most powerful of the bluebird spirits. She began to explain that because of the bitterness of the forest's first and second queens of more than two generations, curses had been made and not all of them were destroyed. These curses could finally be destroyed by the quincunx and the velvet unicorn.

From a distant cloud, women's figures could be seen. Viole's mother and Velve's mother stood face to face, the powers they had were gone. Holding Viole's mother's hand was Violete.

'Violete,' Mauve shouted as he ran towards his daughter. Tears filled his eyes. The mothers of the queens vanished the moment the unicorn lay still.

Mauve returned to the castle, excited to tell Viole and Velve of what had happened. On his return he found Viole and Velve lying on the floor. They were part of the curses the mothers had made. 'Viole! Velve!' Mauve shouted in despair, as tears filled his eyes, whilst holding his daughter in his arms.

Jack At The Zoo

Yvonne Peacock

'Two adults and one child, please,' said Jack's dad as they went through the entrance of the zoo. The man in the kiosk gave Jack the tickets.

'Would you like a zoo guide?'

'Yes please,' said Dad. He paid the man the money and they all went in to the zoo for the day.

'Right then, what would you like to see first?' said Mum.

Jack looked at the guide. 'I want to go and see the elephants.'

They all walked around the path until there in front of them were two really big, grey elephants with long trunks. Mum and Dad sat on a bench and watched Jack as he walked along the side of the enclosure talking to the elephants as they followed him on the other side of the bars.

'Hello elephants, you are very big.' Jack heard a very deep voice.

'Hello, it's nice to meet you. What's your name?'

Jack turned round to see who was talking to him, but there was no one there. 'Over here, I'm over here.' Jack looked around again, but could only see his mum and dad sitting on the bench. 'Coo-ee, I'm over here, over the fence.'

Then Jack realised that the voice was coming from the elephant.

'Hello, my name is Jack and I have never spoken to an elephant before.'

They talked to each other for some time and then Jack said, 'I must go now as I haven't seen any of the other animals.'

'Goodbye Jack, hope to see you again,' said the elephant.

They all went on to see the big cats. Jack ran on and went over to the lion cage.

'Hello, Mr Lion.'

A voice came back. 'Hello, my name is Leo, not Mr Lion.'

'Do all the animals in this zoo talk?' asked Jack.

'Of course they do, but only to children,' said Leo.

Jack took out a pen from his pocket and opened the zoo guide to the big cat cage. He found the picture of the lion. He was very big and proud with a huge, fluffy mane. Jack wrote in the name Leo. 'Could you tell me the names of the elephants?'

Leo said, 'The big one is called Ed and the other is Eve.'

Jack wrote the names in the guide. 'Thank you,' he said and walked on to the next pen.

'Hello,' said a great big, stripy tiger. 'I am pleased to see you, Jack.'

'How do you know my name?' said Jack.

'Ah, all the animals in the zoo know who you are, we have been expecting you.' The tiger told Jack. He was called Indy and went on to explain how he knew Jack. 'When you were small, your mum and dad brought you to the zoo in your pushchair. George the gorilla got out of his cage and took you away. He took you out of your pushchair and climbed up a tree.'

'How did they get me back?' asked Jack.

'Well, you were up the tree for most of the day, but George didn't hurt you. Rilla, the lady gorilla, talked to him and told him to give you back to your mum and dad. George and Rilla's little boy gorilla had been taken to another zoo and they both missed him very much.'

Jack asked Indy if George was still at the zoo.

'Yes,' said Indy. 'He'd be glad to see you after all these years.'

Jack walked on up the path past Bill the buffalo with his two big horns and Camilla the camel who had a great big hump on her back.

They all shouted, 'Hello, Jack.'

He then went past Gill the giraffe with her long neck looking over the fence, Zeb the black and white striped zebra and Karo the kangaroo who was carrying a little baby in her pouch. Boris the wild boar was charging around his pen but came to a halt by the fence to say hello. As Jack walked around the zoo, the animals all shouted hello.

Just then Jack heard a voice shout, 'Jack, are you going to stop for some lunch with us?' It was his mum and dad. They were sitting on a bench with a big picnic basket of food and drink. Jack ran over to them and sat down beside them. Mum gave Jack a piece of pie and a drink of pop.

'Have you finished?' said Mum. 'Would you like a piece of chocolate cake now?'

'Can I save some for George the gorilla? I think he would love your cake, Mum.'

'I think we can spare a little piece,' said Mum.

After lunch Jack said, 'Can I run on to see the rest of the animals?'

Dad said, 'Don't go too far ahead, stay where we can see you.'

Jack ran on past Polly the red and blue parrot and Olly the snow owl.

'Hellooooo,' said Olly.

As he waked past the penguins, they all shouted hello as they waddled over to the fence. Jack looked at the zoo guide and said, 'Only the monkeys now and then the gorillas.'

All the monkeys started to scream. 'Jack's here, Jack's here.'

He went past the monkeys and looked in the next very big cage. There sat the biggest gorilla Jack had ever seen. 'Hello, are you George?' he said.

'I am, and you must be Jack. I'm very glad to see you after all these years.'

Jack went closer to the fence to talk with George. 'Indy the tiger told me how you took me up the tree and that you didn't hurt me,' said Jack. Then Jack asked George where Rilla was.

'She's in the animal hospital, I'm going to be a daddy very soon,' said a happy George.

Jack spent quite a while talking to George about gorillas and the other animals in the zoo. Then he heard his dad shout, 'We have to go soon, Jack. The zoo is going to close soon.'

Jack turned, waved and shouted, 'I'll be there in a moment, I'll just say goodbye to George.' He turned back and said, 'I will come back to see you and Rilla again, and your new little baby.'

George looked sad as Jack walked away with his mum and dad, but he knew that Jack would keep his promise and come to see him one day.

The Day Of The Great Storm

Anna Greaves

Once upon a time, there was a magical island far, far away, in the middle of the deep blue Pacific Ocean. This island was like no other, for it was an island where flowers could breathe, talk and act like people. They lived in families, in pretty houses with dainty gardens. All the flowers lived much longer than people, for it was eternally spring and the island was always beautifully warm.

The sun shone every day and the sky was always blue, except for the odd white rain cloud. Strong winds never blew, but a gentle breeze caressed the flowers' faces and limbs. Dark clouds did not exist. Winter, with its cold and frost, never came! The flower children went to school every day and eventually became adults, but they stayed young for a very long time.

At number ten Primrose Avenue, lived Rosie Rose, the most perfect flower on the island. She was so beautiful that gasps of admiration followed her everywhere she went.

Unfortunately, she was very unkind to others. She thought she was better than them because she knew that she was more beautiful than everyone else. Rosie was also extremely vain. She was so aware of her amazing beauty that she spent most of her time in front of the mirror, admiring herself.

In the house next door lived David Daisy, who was desperately, hopelessly in love with Rosie. He knew that she would never agree to marry him. Actually, she had never even looked at him. David was convinced Rosie had not even noticed that he lived next door, as she was so absorbed by her own beauty.

One day his luck changed. When it rained on the Flower Island, it always did so extremely gently. All the flowers would rush out each time to soak up the warm raindrops, which gave moisture to their dry petals.

On this particular day, something strange happened; something which had never happened before in the history of the island: the sky became suddenly black and it started to *pour down* with great force! Thunder boomed and lightning streaked across the sky! Everyone rushed back into their houses to get away from the violent storm.

Rosie was in the garden before the rain started. She was so busy looking at herself in the mirror, as usual, that she did not notice the sky changing from its perennial blue to a strange, dark colour. So, when the storm started, she was too late to run back into the house. Therefore, her delicate petals were terribly spoilt by the force of the rain and the wind.

The downpour only lasted two minutes. Soon, the sky was blue again and the sun came out. All the flowers rushed out into the streets to talk to each other about the strange storm that had just passed over the island.

Suddenly, Veronica Violet pointed out a strange-looking flower in one of the gardens. 'What a very ugly flower indeed,' Veronica whispered.

Nobody had actually realised that the horrible flower was Rosie. She had turned from being the most beautiful flower on the island into a wet, sloppy, discoloured mess. In two short minutes, she had become the least attractive flower on Earth! One or two of the flowers even started to laugh at what was indeed a sight for sore eyes. As the other flowers laughed, Rosie wept and wept, spoiling her delicate petals even more.

Suddenly, she felt a hand touching her gently on the shoulder and a kind voice talking to her softly.

'You are still the most beautiful flower I have ever seen, Rosie,' the voice said. Rosie looked up timidly, her eyes resting on the handsome, young face of a daisy. 'It's me, David, your neighbour.'

His voice was soothing and his beautiful, brown eyes were full of kindness. Rosie suddenly felt that she was instantly in love with him.

Fortunately, Rosie's ugliness did not last. She soon dried out and regained her beauty. She became a completely different flower, kind and gentle. Rosie was eventually very much loved by all the flowers on the island. She had learnt a very valuable lesson - that beauty does not last and there is much more to someone than good looks.

(Story 1 of 'The Enchanted Island' series)

The Thunder Giants

Rose-Mary Gower

Grown-ups will tell you that thunderstorms are caused by a build-up of electrical charge on the clouds! But ssshhh, can you keep a secret? High in the sky, sitting on a very large, white, fluffy cloud, is a *huge* house which belongs to three giants called Horys, Dorys and their son, Borys.

Everything is so enormous in the giants' house - the chairs, table, sofa, beds and grand piano would seem as high as mountains to you! The only small thing in the giants' house is a very teeny, tiny pet mouse called Morys, belonging to Borys.

Borys has to feed Morys and clean out his cage. Sometimes, like all children, Borys is a bit careless and forgets to shut the cage door. Then Morys escapes and the trouble begins!

In spite of being a very teeny, tiny mouse he has *very* sharp teeth, which he uses to bite through all sorts of things. Morys finds electricity cables very *yummy* indeed.

Suddenly, the lights go out in the giants' house and their white, fluffy cloud goes black. They know that Morys is out of his cage and has chewed through a cable! They have to find him very quickly, before he can cause more damage.

Horys and Dorys tell Borys off for being careless and losing Morys. Giants' voices are like a low rumble! Borys gets very upset when he is scolded and it makes him cry great big teardrops, which fall through the clouds!

As it is dark in the giants' house, they have to get out their large, bright torches. They flash them around to see if Morys is hiding under the furniture. The move the chairs, *crash!* Morys is not there. They move the table, *crash!* Morys is not there. They move the sofa, *crash!* Morys is not there. They move the beds, *crash! Crash! Crash!* Morys is not there! Finally, they move the grand piano, *crash!* But Morys is not there either! Where do you think Morys is? That is right!

While the giants were busy looking for him, Morys had climbed back into his cage and was fast asleep after his adventure!

When the sky gets dark, great big raindrops start to fall and there is a rumbling, a crashing and a flashing. You know that Morys is out of his cage and the giants are looking for him! So don't forget to look at the sky and listen out for the sound of thunder. But we know what is really happening, don't we? Sshhhh, don't tell the grown-ups!

The Adventures Of Hamish

Graham McNicol

Monday: Hamish Makes A New Friend

'Hello, Hamish,' said Jean. Jean is the person Hamish lives with. Hamish is a very large cat, almost a small tiger, golden-brown fur, with black stripes and a very long and bushy tail.

After breakfast, Hamish decided to play in the garden while his tail dried. As he played by the mock orange tree, he looked up at some noisy birds in its branches. As he looked, something dropped from a great height, crashing through the tree, breaking branches as it fell. It hit the grass and bounced, landing at Hamish's feet with what sounded like *'Ouch!'*

Hamish put his head down to smell it.

'G'day,' said a deep voice, 'you're very large for a cat, I'd say almost a small tiger,' said the creature.

Hamish spoke in his best voice, looking down his nose. 'My name is Hamish and this is my garden. Who and what are you?'

The stranger pulled himself up to his full size so that Hamish saw him properly for the first time. Speaking in the same deep voice he said, 'My name is Breadsnapper, I'm a fire-breathing dragon from Australia.'

'Dragons are great big things,' said Hamish, stretching his paws out as if to measure something.

'I'm not; I'm small, I can fly, I can make myself disappear, but I cant make myself any bigger. I'm the size I am and I'm lost with nowhere to stay, but it's nice to be back on the ground. Dragons don't fly very well you know.'

'I know they don't land very well,' said Hamish. 'Are you hungry?'

Breadsnapper yawned. 'I'm tired and hungry. I usually collect bread thrown out for the birds and make toast.'

'I'll bring some cat biscuits, that's all I have. You can sleep under the hedge.' Hamish went to sleep too, not too close - he didn't want his fur to catch fire from his new friend's breath.

Tuesday: Sticky Bottom Hamish

'Hello, Hamish,' said Jean. Jean is the person Hamish lives with. Hamish is a very large cat, almost a small tiger, golden-brown fur, with black stripes and a very long and bushy tail.

As Hamish came into the house, Cameron Jake, Jean's grandson, was going out eating a sticky bun. Now Hamish thought if he was very,

very good, he would become a little boy just like Cameron Jake, but he just couldn't stop chasing birds, catching butterflies and anything else that moved in the garden.

Hamish knew that if he saw anything moving in the garden, his head would go down and his bottom would come up and jiggle about. So he thought if he stopped his bottom from coming up and jiggling about, he would not be able to chase the birds and wouldn't catch the butterflies or anything else that moved in the garden, then he would become a little boy like Cameron Jake.

Later that day, Jean was baking when some of the jam that she was using dropped onto the kitchen floor. Hamish saw his chance - he sat on the jam. It didn't stick his bottom down to the floor as he had hoped, but everywhere he sat became very sticky. Jean had to wash the floor and everything where Hamish had been, including Hamish's bottom, that left his tail very wet.

Wednesday: Hamish's Tantrum

'Hello, Hamish,' said Jean. Jean is the person Hamish lives with. Hamish is a very large cat, almost a small tiger, golden-brown fur, with black stripes and a very long and bushy tail.

As usual, Hamish's tail was wet. He had some breakfast, then rolled up on his chair and went to sleep.

He woke up to hear Jean running a bath. Hamish liked Jean's bath. There were always bubbles and Hamish liked bubbles. He ran up the stairs and into the bathroom. Hamish jumped onto the bath by the taps, a place he liked, he could dangle a paw by the water to catch bubbles without getting wet. He didn't understand why Jean got wet all over, it was the last thing Hamish would do.

This morning, Hamish slipped and went into the bath. The water was hot and it went over his head. He was very frightened. He jumped out when all his paws touched the bottom of the bath. He landed on the floor at the side of the bath, miaowing and shaking his head, then his shoulders shook in the opposite direction, next his back, then his bottom and last of all his tail started to shake, all his body parts going in different directions and stamping his paws.

He ran down the stairs, curled up in front of the heater where he would dry and went to sleep.

When Jean came down the stairs and sat down, Hamish jumped onto her knee for a cuddle, but he was still very wet.

Thursday: Pussy Willow

'Hello, Hamish,' said Jean. Jean is the person Hamish lives with. Hamish is a very large cat, almost a small tiger, golden-brown fur with black stripes, and a very long and bushy tail.

Hamish was not at the door this morning, so Jean looked round the house for him. She could hear Hamish cry, which made her look up and there he was, right at the top of the pussy willow tree that grew in front of the potting shed.

The top branches were as high as the house and very thin - too thin for Hamish's weight. He was stuck, he couldn't go up and he couldn't go down.

Seeing Hamish's problem, the window cleaner made his ladder as long as it would go and put it up to the tree just under Hamish, explaining to Jean that Hamish would know what to do as Hamish often climbed his ladder when he was cleaning windows.

As soon as the ladder was in the correct place, Hamish came running down, his two front paws dropping onto the step below, then the next step, then the next step and then the next step, going faster and faster. Before he got to the bottom, he jumped onto the water barrel. The top of the water barrel slipped to one side and Hamish's tail splashed into the water. Hamish jumped off the water barrel as quickly as possible and ran into the house where he waited for a cuddle, but his tail was too wet.

Friday: The Silver Garden

'Hello, Hamish,' said Jean. Jean is the person Hamish lives with. Hamish is a very large cat, almost a small tiger, golden-brown fur, with black stripes and a very long and bushy tail.

After breakfast, Hamish walked to the bottom of the garden. The garden was covered in a silvery frost that made it sparkle in the bright yellow sunshine.

Hamish had been nice and warm when he had been sat on the roof of Jean's car; his fur had been puffed out with warm air. The door had opened and as he walked into the house, Jean had stroked all the air out of his fur, as he ate his breakfast Hamish had been nice and warm, walking down the path the fresh air in his fur had not warmed up and he felt cold. He ruffled his fur and shook his body.

If he had not had the eyes of a cat, he would not have seen the slight movement in the heather in front of the summer house. Thinking it may be something to play with he went to see what had attracted him.

Sitting on a branch of purple heather, wearing a purple tunic with a purple hat, sat a tiny person with see-through wings.

'Hello, I'm Hamish, who are you?'

'I'm the purple heather fairy. I'm here to bring the colour back to this heather, but my wings are stuck together and I can't fly. I keep slipping off the branches.'

'How can I help?' asked Hamish.

'Breathe on my wings,' said the fairy.

Hamish breathed on her wings and as he did so, the fairy disappeared with a flutter.

Disappointed, Hamish walked back to the kitchen. *She should have said thank you,* he thought as he walked into the kitchen.

'What a beautiful sprig of heather,' said Jean taking the sprig from his ear. 'Is this for me?'

No, thought Hamish, smiling to himself.

Saturday: A Wet Tail

'Hello, Hamish,' said Jean. Jean is the person Hamish lives with. Hamish is a very large cat, almost a small tiger, golden-brown fur, with black stripes and a very long and bushy tail.

When Hamish came into the house in the morning, he liked to jump onto Jean's knee, but because his tail was always wet, Jean would push him off. Hamish missed his morning cuddle, so he ate his breakfast, which Jean had put out for him, then he would sleep away the day, sometimes playing with his toys, or when his tail had dried, sitting on Jean's knee.

He went out at night to play with his friends. When it was morning, he would sit on the wet roof of Jean's car while he waited for Jean to open the door and that is why his tail was always wet and he missed his morning cuddle.

Today, instead of going to sleep after he had eaten his breakfast, he decided to go out and play in the garden.

Earlier, he had noticed that he could see his breath when he breathed out. He hadn't noticed that it was cold with his nice warm coat. He played his usual games, chasing leaves as they were blown from the trees and blown round and round by the wind, then he chased a paper bag that seemed to go faster than the leaves. The bag went up into the sky. Hamish ran and jumped as high as he could, but the bag was too fast for him. The wind blew the bag across the garden pond, leaving Hamish looking into the pond and he saw a cat exactly the same as him looking up at him.

It was Hamish's garden. He felt that if a cat came into his garden, it should ask his permission, or else. Hamish jumped on the cat in the pond. Hamish didn't know that the water in the pond had turned to ice. His two front paws slid from underneath him, his back paws didn't know which way to go, trying to follow the front paws, in something like the same direction.

Hamish went sliding across the pond, bottom stuck up into the air with his tail straight as a maypole and his chin sliding along on the ice. He jumped with all four legs as he came to the other side of the pond, lifting him into the air, breaking the ice and wetting his tail.

He ran home to Jean to have a cuddle, but his tail was too wet, so he curled up as only a cat can and went to sleep on his chair.

Sunday: Disco Mouse Hideout

'Hello, Hamish,' said Jean. Jean is the person Hamish lives with. Hamish is a very large cat, almost a small tiger, golden-brown fur with black stripes and a very long and bushy tail.

As usual, when Hamish came in, he ate his breakfast, but this morning, instead of going to sleep he thought that he would play with Disco mouse. Disco is one of Hamish's toys, covered in different shiny patches, which made the light shine in different ways. He knew exactly where he had left Disco, in the middle of the living room floor where he had played with him last. But when he looked, he wasn't there. He looked at the back of the settee and the back of all the chairs and in the corners of the room, but he wasn't there.

Hamish looked in the wardrobe in the hall. He ran up the stairs and looked into all the bedrooms, going into each wardrobe and all the bedside cupboards. He couldn't find Disco mouse anywhere. He even looked in the bath and behind the toilet, but he wasn't there. He went into the box room, looked all around and even jumped onto the windowsill. He just couldn't find Disco mouse, wherever he looked. So he went downstairs. He was gone and there was nowhere else to look, he decided.

Hamish went into the garden, lay down in the sunniest place in the garden and went to sleep. Whilst Hamish slept, a large black cloud came over and started to rain. Hamish woke up and ran into the house. As he ran through the kitchen, there on top of his toy box sat Disco mouse. *Fancy hiding with all the other toys,* thought Hamish, *no wonder I couldn't find him. I don't want to play with him now.* So he jumped on his chair and went to sleep.

Red Paint

Dorothy M Mitchell

Chapter 1

'Red paint, I just knew we would run out of red paint. Big Elf said we had plenty. I wanted to order more, but he said no.'

Weeks and weeks ago, Chips and Woody Elf, the head carpenters, were counting the amount of fire engines, tractors, lorries and buses wanted for Christmas presents for all the little boys. They said how very busy they were going to be, cutting and carving the toys for this Christmas and they were going to need a lot of red paint.

'You know what Big Elf is like,' said Chips. That's me by the way, Abel Elf. Woody, Chips and myself were very worried.

'If we don't get enough red paint, there will be a lot of unhappy children this year,' said Woody Elf. 'Do you think you could have another word with Big Elf, Abel? We know he's the manager, but you are the supervisor.'

'Well, I will give it a try,' I said, 'but you both know what he's like.'

'Yes,' said Chips Elf, 'a stubborn know-all.'

Now then, as luck had it they didn't have a red paint problem in the part of the toy factory where little girls' toys were made, but Abel Elf thought it worth a try.

'Sorry,' said Archie Elf, the supervisor, 'we don't have much need for red paint. We have lots of pink paint, but somehow I don't think little boys would like pink fire engines and lorries, and have you even seen a pink tractor?' said Archie Elf with a big grin on his face.

I smiled at the thought. 'It's OK, Archie, nice to have had a chat. I am sure a solution will be found. See you.'

Chapter 2

Meanwhile, at the Sack Works, singing could be heard from the elves who were happily working overtime so that enough sacks could be made. Santa Claus had told them all he had a feeling in his bears that it was going to be a very busy time and he would need lots of sacks this year. He loved Christmas, making little girls and boys happy gave him a special glow. The excitement, the snow, the sleigh ride from Lapland to all the towns and villages, visiting the homes of sleeping children all in one night was very hard work, but he loved it, especially when there was a mince pie and a drink of milk left out for him by the children. No wonder he was fat and jolly. It was a good job Rudolph and the other reindeer were strong and the sleigh was a big, sturdy one. It was because of the long journey every year, Santa Claus made sure that Rudolph and all the other reindeer had lots of good hay and plenty of sleep so they would be fit and strong for the long trip.

Chapter 3

'Big Elf had been told that our usual supplier would be closing for two weeks this year, I passed the message to him myself, but did he listen, Chips? No, he didn't. I told you, Abel, he said, we don't need anymore red paint at the moment, we have loads in the stores. But when I went to look, I could only find two tins. What are we going to do, Chips? Santa will be so upset. We can't let all the children down. What are we going to do?' I looked at Chips and Woody Elf. They were as worried as me.

'I think we will have to ask Santa. He will work something out,' Woody said to us both.

So off we went to see Santa. We found him having a snooze in his grotto. He needed a good rest before the long journey on Christmas Eve.

'What is it, Abel Elf? You three look so worried.'

We explained to Santa what had happened - about there not being enough red paint. 'I think I had better have a word with Big Elf,' said Santa, 'try not to worry.'

When Big Elf realised how wrong he had been, he had a very red face. 'I am so sorry, Santa, it is all my fault.' He looked at me. 'I should have listened to you, Abel.'

'Well, it seems you have learned your lesson,' said Santa, 'so we must put our thinking caps on and try to come up with a plan.'

Chapter 4

'We could try the Goodlux factory in Toytown,' I said.

'The only trouble is, I don't think Rudolph will be able to find his way,' said Santa. 'It's a long way, right around the back of the moon and on past the highest mountain in Neverland. He won't make it on his own, the other reindeer haven't been either. But leave it with me, I think I know who will help.' With that, Santa left his grotto and went around to the lake.

Silver Mist was sitting on his nest with his wife, Sparkle, a most handsome pair of swans.

'Hello you two,' said Santa.

'Hello, sir,' said Silver Mist. 'Can we help you?'

'Well I hope you can,' said Santa. 'We have a big problem.'

Santa explained what the trouble was. Silver Mist and Sparkle listened to what Santa Claus had to say.

'No wonder you have been worried, so close to Christmas Eve and the long journey from Lapland to every town and village. You poor thing, I can see why Abel, Chips and Woody were concerned. It will be terrible if sufficient red paint can't be found, but please tell the others that I do know the way to the Goodlux factory. It is on the way to Toy Town, past the dark side of the moon and straight on till we get there.'

'Oh, Silver Mist, how can I ever thank you?' said Santa with relief in his voice. 'I will go and give Abel and the others the good news, but first I must go and give Rudolph and the other reindeer the news.'

Rudolph gave a big sigh, 'You say Silver Mist can lead the way to the Goodlux factory? Oh, that's wonderful, Santa,' said Rudolph.

Big Elf said to Abel, 'Will you give the foreman at the Goodlux factory a ring and make sure they have enough red paint before we go any further?' He had made a bad mistake concerning the red paint and he didn't want anything else to go wrong.

Abel rang the factory, 'Can I speak to the boss, please?'

'Speaking,' said a friendly voice.

'I wonder if you can help,' said Abel and he explained the situation.

'Yes, I am sure we will be able to provide as much red paint as you require. When can we expect you?' said the Goodlux boss.

'Let me check with Santa Claus and I will get back to you.'

By this time everyone at the paint works knew about the red paint problem. It was the talk of the place.

'Let's hope Big Elf has learned a valuable lesson,' were the words echoing round the paint works. 'It doesn't do to be too clever and a know-all.'

Chapter 5

I was happy to report back to Santa that the Goodlux factory was able to supply us with the amount of red paint we required.

'Oh, that's good, Abel. What smashing news. We must hurry and prepare everything for the journey. I think we should use the biggest sleigh, don't you, Abel?'

I agreed with Santa. It was also decided that as the cargo would be very heavy and strength would be needed, Santa would ask big Frosty, the snowman, to lend a hand.

'Oh, I would love to help,' said Frosty. He loved Santa. 'Anyway, it would be a lovely ride in the crisp, cold air.'

It was also decided that Big Elf should be allowed to go. Well, he was sorry and he was also big and strong. As I am only a little elf, Silver

Mist said I could ride on his back. Wasn't it all exciting? Santa asked Woody and Chips if they would like to go with us, but they said, 'Is it alright if we stay here and prepare the toys for painting?'

Santa said, 'That's fine. It's up to you, I know how busy you are at the moment. And are you quite sure about riding on Silver Mist's back, Abel? It's a long way and you will have to hold on very tight.'

'Oh, I will be fine,' I assured Santa.

'Don't worry,' said Silver Mist, 'Abel will be quite safe with me.'

It was decided that as everything was arranged and it was going to be a full moon tomorrow night, that the adventure could begin then. I was shaking with excitement.

Rudolph said, 'I don't think I will sleep a wink tonight.'

Silver Mist was as calm as you like. 'Just take it in your stride, it's always the best way.'

I thought Silver Mist was quite right, so I tried to calm myself down and get some sleep. Tomorrow would soon be here.

Chapter 6

It was morning at last. The adventure was almost here. It was decided we would set off when the moon was full and the sky quiet, all the birds asleep in their nests, as little distraction as possible.

I said to Silver Mist, 'It looks like it's going to be a clear night so the stars will be out.'

'You are quite right, Abel, they will help to light our way.'

So after making a phone call to the boss at the Goodlux factory to tell him we were just about to set off, we took our positions. Big Elf and Frosty the snowman climbed aboard the sleigh and while Santa got Rudolph and the other reindeer harnessed to the sleigh, making sure Rudolph's light was shining bright, I climbed onto Silver Mist's back and wriggled about until I felt comfortable. Then, with a wave to Santa, we were off, climbing higher and higher above the trees and into the open sky.

'Wow, what a take-off,' said Big Elf. 'my tummy is doing cartwheels.'

Frosty said, 'Oh, this is lovely. Nice and cold.'

'Are you alright, Abel?' Silver Mist asked.

'I'm fine thanks. I was just thinking to myself what a lucky elf I am. This is some adventure. If I hadn't needed red paint, I wouldn't be doing this.'

All that could be heard was the whoosh of Silver Mist's wing, the snorting noise of Rudolph's breathing and the gallop of reindeer legs as we continued on the long journey to the Goodlux factory. It was magic. On and on we travelled, Rudolph's light glowing bright red and reindeer legs galloping after Silver Mist and me through the night sky.

I think I must have fallen asleep for a while because as I looked down now, it was beginning to get light. I could make out green fields and what looked like a town.

Silver Mist said, 'I think I can see Toy Town, Abel, Will you give Rudolph a shout?'

'OK,' I said. 'Rudolph, hey Rudolph, Toy Town below.'

'Thank you, Abel,' said Rudolph. 'We won't be long now.'

'No,' I said, 'how are you feeling, Rudolph?'

'My legs are a bit tired, but I feel fine thank you Abel.'

Soon we were gliding over the Goodlux factory. Swooping down, Silver Mist and me landed in a large yard, Rudolph and the others close behind.

'You made it then. Did you have a pleasant journey?'

'Very smooth, thank you.' We shook hands.

'I'm Ernest Elf, the foreman. They all call me the boss, in fun of course. I don't mind, they're a good bunch of elves. When they heard about your trouble regarding the red paint problem, they made sure enough was made. Like I said, they are a smashing bunch. Refreshments have been prepared for you all, if you would follow me to the canteen.'

'Oh, can I stay outside, please?' It was Frosty the snowman. 'If I go indoors I will melt!'

'OK Frosty, stay by the door and I will bring you an icicle to suck and the reindeer can go to the barn where they will find sweet hay and cool water. If the rest of you make your way to the canteen, you will be served with a hot meal and drinking chocolate.'

'Oh, thank you Ernest,' said Big Elf.

'And for you, Silver Mist, our cook made a lovely bread pudding.'

So, when everyone had enjoyed their meal and had a nice rest, Ernest Elf said, 'OK Abel, I will go and ask the toy workers to bring the amount of red paint you require. Woolly Bear and Ezra Elephant are very strong, I will go and call them.'

So while Big Elf and me hitched Rudolph and the other reindeer to the sleigh, Woolly Bear and Ezra Elephant stacked all the red paint, securely boxed and tied with strong rope, onto the floor of what Woolly Bear called a Big Cart. Frosty and Big Elf climbed aboard. I jumped onto Silver Mist's back and wriggled until I was comfortable. So, with waving and thanks all round, we set off once more.

'Are you OK, Abel?' Silver Mist asked.

'Yes, I'm fine thank you, sat between these strong wings I feel very secure.'

'Are you OK, Rudolph?' I asked. The deer nodded. I thought how extra bright his red light was shining. He must be happy that we were at last on our way home with the precious cargo.

Chapter 7

'You made it then. We have all been looking at the sky, waiting for your return.'

It was Santa Claus and what looked like every elf in Lapland, cheering and clapping. The sack work singers welcomed us with a selection of Christmas carols.

'Did you have a good journey?' said Santa.

'It was wonderful,' I said. 'If Big Elf hadn't made that mistake, we wouldn't have had the adventure, so all's well that ends well.'

I think Woody and Chips Elf were the most relieved of all that they had at last got enough red paint. 'We will just about have time to finish the fire engines, tractors and lorries before Santa goes on his long journey on Christmas Eve,' they told me.

I thought to myself it had really been a wonderful adventure. Silver Mist with his beautiful, strong wings, Rudolph and his bright light following him, the other reindeer galloping behind, all pulling the huge sleigh carrying the precious cargo of red paint, not forgetting Frosty the snowman and Big Elf, especially Big Elf. If it hadn't been for him, we wouldn't have had all the excitement of the lovely journey to the Goodlux factory to get red paint.

Optimus Sprott Goes To School

Ann-Lowry Fearon

When Optimus Sprott cut off his little sister Ottilie's pigtails with the big kitchen scissors, old Mrs Peabody next door said to his mum, 'It's time that boy was in school!'

When Optimus Sprott ate all the ice cream, topped off with a handful of chocolate biscuits, and was then very sick all over the floor of the hall closet, where he was hiding, his mum said to his dad, 'Oh well! At least he will soon be in school.'

When Optimus Sprott went to his friend Sammy's house and let all Sammy's big brother's rabbits out of their cages, his dad said to Sammy's mother, 'We're hoping he will get better once he goes to school.'

Optimus thought, *I don't like the sound of this. I don't need to be made better as I am perfectly all right as I am, so I won't go to school. I'll stay at home instead and carry on eating ice cream and chocolate biscuits.*

But something was afoot!

First of all, Optimus was taken by his mum to the children's school outfitters in the high street, where he was fitted out with a purple blazer, grey trousers, grey and purple socks and a grey jumper.

Next he found himself at the stationers, where his mum bought a pencil, a pencil case, a rubber, a ruler, a smart red and yellow backpack and a packet of felt-tip pens.

Lastly, they went to the supermarket, where his mum bought a Spider-Man lunchbox, an apple, a crusty roll, some cheese, some ham, some raisins and a carton of orange juice.

By bedtime, Optimus had decorated the walls of his bedroom with wonderful felt-tip pen drawings, and the felt-tip pens had been taken away from him. And the next morning, before he had had time to get up to any mischief, he was on his way to school.

The school yard was full of other boys and girls, all wearing purple blazers and all carrying backpacks or satchels and lunchboxes. A bell rang and a very tall lady appeared and said, 'Line up everybody. New children come with me.'

I'm a new children, thought Optimus Sprott, *but I won't go with her. She's scary!*

He turned to look for his mum but she seemed to have disappeared, and the school gate was closed. There was no escape.

Maybe if I try very hard I can cope with this thing, he thought. *After all, it's only for one day. I'm five now, and I'm very brave, and I won't have to come back tomorrow!*

Then the tall scary lady scooped him up and soon he found himself in a big, sunny classroom, with just-the-right-size tables and chairs and a pretty lady, wearing a lovely red jumper and a big smile.

'My name is Miss Cherry and I am your new teacher,' the pretty lady said. 'I would like you all to come and sit on this big mat beside my chair while I tell you about all the wonderful things that you are going to learn to do in school.

Optimus found himself sitting beside a little girl with long pigtails, just like his sister's. His sister had been very pleased when he cut off her pigtails with the big kitchen scissors. Probably this little girl would be pleased too. He looked round for some big scissors, but there did not seem to be any. Then he remembered that his mum and dad had not been pleased about the pigtails. In fact, they had been extremely cross, so cross that they had told Optimus he could not have any ice cream for a week! Maybe pretty Miss Cherry would be cross. Maybe she would tell the tall scary lady about him and she would be cross too and would tell Optimus he could not have any ice cream ever again. Maybe he would forget about the scissors!

Optimus had not been listening to Miss Cherry, but now he heard her say, 'Now, children, you may choose whether you want to play in the Wendy house or the sandpit, or take out the building toys or read in the book corner, or whether you would like to make me a lovely painting. But if you are painting, you must wear a painting apron in case you make a mess.'

Optimus looked round the classroom. He saw the book corner and the Wendy house. He saw the sandpit, where some boys were already digging. He saw the wooden easels and the big tubs of brightly-coloured paint. Painting, he decided. *That's what I want to do.* In no time at all he had painted a wonderful splashy thunderstorm painting, and his hands, his face and even the front of his jumper.

Miss Cherry came to look.

'That's a lovely painting, Optimus,' she said kindly. 'You're quite an artist, aren't you? Would you like to paint another picture while I hang this one up to dry? We'll just put this apron on you, so you don't make a mess.'

Optimus painted two more splashy thunderstorm paintings. He painted the floor a bit too, and part of the wall, and then his hand sort of slipped and he found he was painting the little girl with the pigtails as well.

'Whoops!' said Miss Cherry, deftly removing the paintbrush and giving the little girl with the pigtails a bit of a wipe. 'Would you like to help me wash the brushes now, Optimus? It's nearly time for lunch.'

At lunch, Optimus flicked a raisin at a boy called Billy. Billy flicked it back. Then Optimus flicked it again and Billy ate it. Then Billy lobbed half a hard-boiled egg at Optimus. Yeugh! He wasn't eating that! He threw it back, but it didn't hit Billy. It hit the little girl with the pigtails.

'That's quite enough of that you two,' said Miss Cherry firmly, picking up the hard-boiled egg and consoling the little girl, who had started to cry. 'Hurry up, do. It's time to go out to play.'

'Want a fight?' Billy asked Optimus when they found themselves in the playground.

'Ooh yes!' said Optimus, and soon they were happily scuffling and rolling about on the floor.

'Stop that!' It was the tall scary lady. She hauled Optimus and Billy to their feet. 'You should be ashamed of yourself, Billy Biggs! Now say sorry at once,' she instructed, 'then go and wait inside until the end of playtime.'

Billy draped his arm around Optimus's shoulder as they trailed inside.

'We'll do it again tomorrow,' he whispered. 'We'll hide behind the bike shelter. She won't spot us there!'

I won't be here tomorrow, thought Optimus, feeling a little sad, but he didn't say anything because he had just noticed a big cage on the cupboard in the corner of the classroom. Something small, fluffy and golden with big black eyes and a woffly sort of nose was looking out at him, clutching the bars of the cage with its tiny front paws. *It's asking me to let it out of there,* thought Optimus.

He started to open the cage.

'Don't do that!' said Billy in alarm. 'That's Goldy, our hamster, that is. Didn't you hear Miss Cherry say that he has to stay in his cage in case he gets lost?'

Then Optimus remembered Sammy's big brother's rabbits. It had taken all afternoon to catch them, and everyone had been very hot and bothered and cross. That time had had not had any ice cream for a fortnight. Perhaps after all Goldy the hamster would be happier staying in his cage ... He took his hand away from the latch.

'It's quite good here, isn't it?' said Billy. 'I haven't got a hamster at my house, and I haven't got anyone to fight with either.'

Optimus thought about his house. He didn't have a hamster, or any paints or a sandpit, and he was definitely not allowed to fight with his little sister. In fact, now that he thought about it, he had not had so much fun in ages. But what about the tall scary lady?

'I don't like that tall scary lady,' he whispered to Billy.

Billy began to laugh. He laughed so hard that for a little while he was quite unable to speak, and had to roll around on the floor to make the words come out.

'That's my Auntie Dottie,' he finally managed to splutter. 'She's just the school seckertary. You don't want to be frightened of her. She won't hurt you, and anyway, she's lovely when you get to know her!'

'Oh that's all right then,' said Optimus. 'In that case I'll be quite sorry when school is over. I wonder what Mum and Dad have got planned for me tomorrow.'

'You'll be here tomorrow, silly,' Billy told him. 'You have to come to school every day. Well, not Saturday or Sunday or Christmas Day or at Easter, of course, but every other day. We'll be able to have a fight every day! Won't that be good!'

And they rolled on the floor and scuffled and kicked until the bell went.

'And what did you learn at school today, Optimus?' Dad asked him later.

'Oh nothing yet,' said Optimus, 'but I expect I will learn lots of things tomorrow.'

The Rainbow Puddle

Julie Deeks

Splooshhhhh! Seren was up to her wellies in puddle water again. But, right up ahead, there was an even better puddle to muddy herself in. With her tongue hanging out of the side of her mouth, she took a good run up ready to launch, but stopped just as she reached the new puddle.

'Oh look, Connor,' she whispered to her little brother who was also all puddly, 'a rainbow!'

Connor looked to where Seren was pointing. Right there, in the middle of the puddle, were red and yellow and green and pink and blue and purple and orange and indigo and violet - a beautiful rainbow.

'Wow,' gasped Connor.

'Let's splash!' shouted Seren, 'after three - one ... two ...' *splooooosssshhhh!*

The two children leapt straight in, splishing and splashing the rainbow as hard as they could with their wellies, until it was all sploshed away.

Suddenly, all the rainbow colours seemed to lift up out of the puddle and fill the air, swirling and whirling all around them. Seren and Connor stopped splashing and watched, aghast as the beautiful colours whooshed and swished past their ears, tickling their noses and making their hair stand up on tiptoe.

Slowly, the colours became sparkles and started to fall like rain back to the ground. As they fell, they formed the shape of a teeny, tiny little person.

'W ... w ... what is that?' whispered Connor - his mouth hanging open. Seren was just about to ask the same question when the little being spoke.

'*It*? ... What is *it*?' she harrumphed - sounding more than a bit angry, 'I'm not an *it,* I'm a fairy. And it's about time too. I thought you were never coming.' And with that she folded her arms in front of her and glared hard at the two shocked children. Seren couldn't help but giggle.

'A fairy!' she said, sniggering, 'you're not a fairy! Fairies have beautiful wings and sparkling dresses and crowns and wands - not muddy dungarees and welly boots!'

The angry fairy raised an eyebrow. 'What's wrong with my dungarees?' she huffed. 'And who says fairies have to have sparkly dresses?'

Seren looked at the tiny, cross fairy and thought for a second. 'Well, in all my books ...'

'*Humpphh!*' snorted the fairy in disgust, 'shows what *you* know!' she said, stomping a tiny welly on the wet ground.

'Look - I'm sorry,' said Seren feeling a bit guilty. 'I've just never met a real live fairy before. I don't even know your name,' and with that she reached down to let the fairy step onto her hand.

'Doris,' said the fairy, blowing her straggly hair out of her eyes. 'And you are ...?'

'Seren,' said Seren curtseying prettily, 'and this is my little brother Connor.' Connor grinned a toothy grin and shook Doris' tiny fingers a little too hard.

'Whoah! Careful!' wobbled Doris, almost plopping off the end of Seren's hand. Connor and Seren couldn't help but chuckle, but Seren gave Doris her finger to hold onto, so she could get her balance.

'What were you doing in a muddy puddle?' said Seren suddenly. 'It's hardly the place for a fairy, is it?'

Doris looked sad. 'I was banished from the Fairy Kingdom,' she said unhappily, flopping down onto her bottom and crossing her legs. 'The Great Fairy Princess said I was a disgrace to all fairies, and until I learn to use my wand and wings properly, I can't go back. So I had to wait for someone to break the rainbow and release me.'

'Wow,' said Seren, 'so what happens now? Can you go home?'

'Weren't you listening?' snapped Doris, scratching some mud off a tatty wing, 'I can't go back until I can fly and do all that wand stuff.'

Seren looked thoughtfully at her. 'So how are you meant to learn?'

'Well that's your job, isn't it?' said Doris, impatiently. 'You broke the rainbow - so you have to teach me, *obviously.'*

Seren and Connor looked at each other worriedly and then turned back to a very stroppy Doris.

'You'd better come with us, then,' shrugged Seren, not really knowing what else to say.

'Right,' said Seren, standing in the bathroom back at home, 'first of all, let's get all this mud off you.'

Doris stared at her and frowned. '*How?* And *what for?*' Seren filled the sink with hot water and bubble bath.

'*Please* tell me you've had a bath before!'

'*No!*' sneered Doris looking in disgust at the bubbles. 'Why? *Should* I have?'

'Yeuch!' said Seren, showing her obvious disgust, 'our mum makes us have baths all the time.' Doris wasn't convinced.

'Just get in,' persuaded Seren, 'it's fun, really.'

Holding onto her dungarees, Doris slid into the sink.

'*Aaaaaahhhhhttttcccchhhhooooooooo!*' The bubbles had tickled Doris' nose. She sneezed so hard that she shot across the sink and bumped her head on the taps. 'Fun?' glared the soggy fairy rubbing her sore head.

Finally, Doris was clean and Seren gave her a dry flannel to use as a towel. Then, sitting the fairy on her dressing table, Seren set about combing her wet hair out of her eyes. Before Doris could see what she was doing, Seren had plugged in the hairdryer and was fiddling with the switch.

'Erm ... what's *thaaaaaaaaaaaaaagggggggghhhhhhh?*'

Whhhhhoooooossshhhhh! The hot air blew Doris straight across the dressing table and ... *boinnnngg!* she landed with a bounce on Seren's bed.

'*Oops!*' said Seren, scooping a very dizzy Doris back up again, 'Sorry!'

'Watch it,' grumbled the fairy, smoothing down her sticky-up hair.

'I'll just tie it up for you,' said Seren, quickly knotting Doris' long hair into a bun. 'Now, let's start with the wand. Can you do *any* magic?' Doris thought for a moment.

'I turned my brother into a penguin once,' she replied, looking pleased with herself. Seren stared at her.

'Have you *got* a wand?' she asked, looking more than just a bit scared.

Doris nodded and pulled out a broken stick, with what looked like a half chewed star hanging off the top.

'Is *that* it?' cringed Seren, who was starting to get used to being shocked. Doris saw the look on Seren's face.

'What's wrong with it?' frowned the fairy.

'I'll fetch the Sellotape,' said Seren.

Rummaging in her art box, Seren fished out some paint, glue, glitter and Sellotape. Then, with some 'help' from her little brother, they set about trying to turn the battered old stick into a real fairy wand. 'There!' announced Seren finally, waving the mended wand grandly.

Doris looked up from trying to unstick her fingers from one another. 'Wow!' she whispered, taking the wand carefully from her new friend, 'it's beautiful!'

Seren smiled down at her. 'Glad you like it. Let's hope it doesn't do wonky magic anymore.'

'Well - let's try?' said Doris eyeing Connor, who was busy putting the Sellotape away.

'No penguins,' warned Seren. Doris smiled.

The wand worked perfectly and within a few minutes, Doris had magicked up a whole feast for the three of them. There were jam sandwiches, strawberry milkshakes with wiggly straws, chocolate raisins and, of course, fairy cakes. Seren, Connor and Doris munched hungrily.

'Can we keep her?' whispered Connor through a mouthful of cake.

'It would be nice wouldn't it,' replied Seren, thoughtfully. 'I wonder if she could magic me a new bike!' Seren chuckled, then shook her head, 'but no - she has to go back to her family in the Fairy Kingdom.'

Connor looked sad and slurped the rest of his milkshake down noisily.

Seren turned back to Doris who was covered in chocolate and crumbs. 'How do we teach you to fly then?' Doris dusted herself down and shrugged her shoulders.

'Maybe now my wings are clean, they'll work a bit better,' she said, admiring them proudly in the mirror. Seren nodded.

'Can you try?' she asked. Doris shrugged again and stood up, stretching her now shining wings. There was a tiny buzzing sound as slowly, her wings flapped and she lifted up into the air. Up, up, up she went, carefully at first, then a little faster. She zoomed around the light, then swooped down over the bed and fluttered just above the children who laughed and clapped happily.

Doris looked very pleased with herself and zipped across the room to the door then soared, whizzing straight towards the window.

Splat!

Doris crashed in a star shape and slid squeakily down the glass, landing in a crumpled heap on the window sill.

'Doris!' squealed Seren, dashing to the dazed fairy.

'I'm fine,' slurred Doris, pulling herself up. She patted at her face to make sure her nose was still there then rubbed at the giant red bump that was appearing on her forehead.

'This is going to take a lot of practise,' said Seren in her most serious voice.

Two days and some very sore bruises later, Doris could land beautifully. She could even do it on one leg - almost like a ballerina she thought. Seren looked proudly at her friend as she practised one last time.

'Are you sure you don't want to put a dress on?' said Seren holding up a purple tutu that belonged to a now naked dolly. Doris glared at her. She still didn't understand what was wrong with her dungarees. Seren shrugged. 'Well, Doris, I think you're ready!'

'I think I am,' smiled the fairy, nodding.

'Oh,' said Seren, suddenly worried, 'how do you get back? You can't go in the puddle again, you're all clean!' Doris shook her head.

'No - all I have to do is ring my fairy bell. If it works, then it means I'm ready and the other fairies will come and get me.'

Seren looked sad. 'We'll miss you, Doris.'

'Oh, I'll still be around,' replied the fairy, tugging playfully at Seren's laces, 'whenever you see a rainbow, that'll be me saying hi.'

Seren looked happier as she carefully lifted Doris up into her hand.

Doris reached deep into her pocket and pulled out a shiny gold bell. Holding it out in front of her, she nervously shook it back and forth. It tinkled so daintily that Seren could hardly hear it. Doris was smiling happily.

'It works!' she shouted, 'I can go home!'

'Do you really have to go?' sniffed Connor, sadly. Doris flew down next to Connor's face and planted a big, sloppy fairy kiss right on his cheek.

'Yuk!' said Connor, wrinkling his nose up.

Suddenly the room was filled with sparkles and beautiful colours.

'It's them!' laughed Doris, flying around the room. She came to a stop in front of Seren, fluttering in mid-air.

'I'll never forget how you helped me become a true fairy,' she smiled. 'Thank you for being such a kind friend.'

Seren smiled back. 'It was our pleasure,' she whispered.

'Don't forget to look for the rainbows,' shouted Doris as she darted up to the ceiling. And then, with a giant *puff!* of fairy dust and a flash of wellies, she was gone. Seren and Connor gazed around the room sadly, as the fairy dust slowly disappeared.

'Seren! Connor! Can you come here please?' shouted their mum from downstairs. Connor followed his big sister sadly to the kitchen, where their mum was waiting for them. 'Can either of you two explain this?' she frowned, opening the back door.

The children looked confused. There, on the patio stood a very large strawberry milkshake with a wiggly straw. Next to it was the most beautiful pink and lilac bicycle that Seren had ever seen. Laughing, Seren and Connor ran outside.

'Thanks, Doris!' they shouted, waving up to the rainbow, which had just appeared in the blue summer sky.

The Unhappy Clown

Nola B Small

Tuff-Tuff the clown had a problem. Aren't clowns supposed to be jolly and joyful? Well, Tuff-Tuff was not! He could not laugh. He was fine whilst he was doing his circus routine but when he had finished, the tears ran down his face.

When the circus came to town the children flocked to the Big Tent to get excitement. They loved the trapeze, the acrobats, the jugglers who juggled glitzy balls and the bareback riders. They also loved the seals and dogs who did tricks and cheered after their acts finished. But, best of all, they loved the clown with his baggy trousers, brightly-painted face and floppy hat with pom-poms on it. He was the favourite. How they laughed at his tricks and acrobatics!

Best of all, they exploded with laughter when he did a handstand and lost his balance, fell off the pony or his bicycle would break-up and he'd fall.

Underneath his bright and happy make-up Tuff-Tuff was not laughing. He saw nothing funny in his falling off a horse or having cold water poured over him, on a cold day.

The circus troupe decided that they had to cheer him up. The ringmaster said, 'Let's make his costume brighter. Let's try yellow and red - not white!'

So they did that but Tuff-Tuff was still sad.

'Let us do some tricks, just for him,' said the ponies. 'Let's stand up on our back legs.' But Tuff-Tuff did not laugh. He did not even smile.

Then the ringmaster said, 'I know! There is nothing a clown likes better than having someone to play tricks upon.' So they put in a second clown - Tiffle. As well, he suggested that Tuff-Tuff should ask someone in the audience to come in the ring - a child or an adult then he could play a trick on them. The audience liked that, he remembered, when he worked for another circus.

The circus arrived at the next town and it was time for Tuff and Tiffle's act. Tuff-Tuff tried to juggle a custard pie and it fell right on Tiffle's head. A smile came over Tuff-Tuff's face when he saw Tiffle. Then he washed a window and threw the bucket of water away, hitting poor Tiffle. Great chuckles of laughter came from the children and Tuff-Tuff broke into giggles. Then Tiffle knocked over a paint-pot, colouring his shoes and trousers. The crowd roared and so did Tuff-Tuff.

Finally, he asked a boy to come out of the audience. He did some kind of magic, vanishing trick with a pigeon. The boy and audience were amazed. Tuff-Tuff was very pleased with himself.

The crowd thought that the two clowns were much better than one and they cheered and hooted. Tuff-Tuff felt good. He was now a happy, smiling clown and he was never sad, again.

Frederick And The Magic Flute

June Worsell

Down in the garden pond, a little cloud slipped quietly among the reeds, and if you had looked closer, you would have seen that the cloud was made up of hundreds of tiny tadpoles swimming about happily.

Each day the tadpoles grew a little bigger until they started to grow arms and legs, lose their tails and look more like their mother, who was of course a frog. However, one very small tadpole had not finished growing his legs and was a different colour from his brothers and sisters.

Mummy frog, had named all of her children 'Freddy' (even the girls), which is a very common name for frogs. The reason for this was that when she called them to her it was far easier to call one name, otherwise, calling them all different names would have taken a very long time indeed.

'Freddy,' she called, and all the baby frogs came from everywhere to find out what Mummy wanted. 'My dears,' she said, 'the time has come for all of you to leave home pond and find you own way in the world. All except Frederick, who has not finished growing his legs yet.'

Why did she call one little frog 'Frederick' you may ask. Was it that he was small, and had turned the brightest shade of green you ever saw?

Although he was not quite a complete frog, he always managed to get into trouble. He was not a naughty frog, just very clumsy and he did not croak but yelled *'Scroak!'* in the loudest voice that you ever heard, which made everyone jump, and if you happen to be a frog, that's very, very high.

He frightened the ducks, the newts, the dragonflies, even the birds in the trees. That's why he was the only one Mummy frog called the full name of 'Frederick'.

He was so unhappy when all his brothers and sisters said goodbye and sat down on a lily pad watching them all hop away.

'Scroak!' he cried.

'Don't do that,' said a voice from somewhere high up in a tree.

'My, my,' said Blackbird as it flew down and landed on the ground just in front of Frederick.

'Please don't say scroak again. What's the matter? Why are you crying?' asked Blackbird, 'but please don't answer scroak, it frightens me.'

So Frederick told the blackbird how he had been left behind because he had not grown his legs properly. 'I'm also, this luminous colour of green, still have a tail and can't stop myself from saying *Scroak!*'

'No! No! No! You've just said it, now I'm bound to have a headache,' said Blackbird trying to cover his ears with his wings.

Blackbird tried to think of something nice to say but he couldn't, everything Frederick had said was true.

'I wish I had a pretty voice like you Blackbird, you sing so beautifully.'

'Why don't you learn how to play a musical instrument?' said Blackbird, whilst busy pulling a fat juicy worm out of the soil, 'then you won't have to talk or sing.'

'*Scroak!*' said Frederick excitedly.

Poor Blackbird dropped his worm in fright, and flew off over the garden sounding his alarm call.

Oh dear thought Frederick *I've done it again, I am a silly frog, I wonder what a musical instrument can be?* He hopped away on his new legs. Legs! New legs! At last they had grown! Frederick had spent so much time feeling sorry for himself he had not noticed them, or that his tail had gone. He spent the rest of the day jumping around trying out his new legs.

The next morning, Frederick came upon a robin who was sitting on a fence singing. 'Hi Robin,' said the little green frog, 'you know a lot about music, could you please tell me where I could buy a musical instrument?'

'If I do, please don't yell *scroak,*' said Robin.

'I promise,' replied Frederick.

'Try Otter's Music Shop down by the river, it's a pity you can't fly, it's a long way, and don't forget to tell your mum where you are going.'

The little green frog became so excited that he forgot his promise to Robin. '*Scroak!*' he yelled, and Robin flew away leaving a flurry of red and brown feathers behind him.

'I'm glad you have your legs at last Frederick,' his mummy said when he told her of his quest in search of a musical instrument. 'One word of caution before you go, beware of Heron, he's rather fond of eating little frogs, and I almost forgot you will need some money.' With that she handed him a whole £50.

Frederick said goodbye and left home pond. He was a big frog now, how all of his friends would admire him when he could play a musical instrument. He had been hopping along for some time, when he began to feel very tired. He had reached the river but still had a long journey ahead of him.

Before he arrived at Otter's Music Shop, Frederick decided to have a rest. He sat down between two tall trees. No sooner had he closed his eyes than he felt one of the trees move.

Startled, he jumped up and his eyes travelled up what he believed to be tree trunks, but instead they disappeared into a mass of grey feathers. 'Heron,' Frederick yelled, then *'Scroak!'* so loudly that Heron immediately spread its large wings and flew away, calling back, 'I could not eat anything as noisy and green as you!'

Frederick set off again along the river bank and after a while came upon a little sign which read *Otter's Music Shop*. He was so pleased at having found the shop he very nearly let out another *scroak!* He had to bite his lip hard to stop himself. He cautiously peeped inside. All around were violins, banjos, clarinets, trumpets and every musical instrument that you could imagine. In the corner on the floor, stood an elegant harp, a double bass, a cello and some large kettle drums.

Frederick went inside and hopped up to the wooden counter.

'What can I do for you little green frog?' came a very deep voice from behind it.

It was Otter and Frederick thought he looked rather fierce, for the animal had just been swimming in the river and his fur was wet and flattened.

Otter smiled at him, revealing his sharp pointed teeth. 'Come closer,' said Otter, 'I won't eat you. You're far too green to be edible.'

Frederick hopped forward, still a little nervous, 'I have come to buy a musical instrument, because I have a terrible voice, not at all like other frogs. Blackbird said if I were to play a musical instrument, it could be my new voice and I will sing like the birds.'

'Can you play anything at all?' said Otter.

'No not yet but I want to learn, you have so many instruments I don't know which to choose!'

Otter smiled, 'Perhaps you would like to try some to see which you feel comfortable with, but please practise outside on the bank as beginners give me a headache.'

'Oh please may I try that drum first of all?'

Otter and Frederick carried the big drum outside, where the little green frog was given two drumsticks.

As Otter turned and went back into his shop, Frederick began to play the drum. *Boom, boom, boom, boom* until he made so much noise, that the ground began to shake. it was deafening, it was even louder than *'Scroak!'*

Very soon a grumpy old mole popped up from under the ground. 'Stop it! Stop it! this minute,' he cried, but Frederick couldn't hear him and kept on banging the drum.

Boom, boom, even louder *boom, boom!*

Otter who heard the commotion, rushed out of his shop and quickly removed the drumsticks from Frederick's hands. Suddenly it all went quiet.

'Sorry Mole, I don't think a drum is such a good idea, come Frederick, let's find something else for you to play.'

'I'd like to try that huge violin please Otter,' said Frederick.

'It's called a cello and you will need some music and a music stand. The music is there to tell you what to play.' Otter showed Frederick how to hold the cello and bow and pointed to the written music.

'It looks easy,' said the little green frog. 'It's frog language, see the little tadpoles climbing up a fence.'

'Silly frog,' mumbled Otter, 'they are not tadpoles, they are called crochets, quavers and minims. That's not a fence but staff lines. That's how music is written.'

Frederick proved to be very good at the cello and soon began to play gentle but sad music. It was so sad, that a party of swans that were swimming by on the river soon fell under its spell. It wasn't very long before the swans began to cry.

'Please stop, dear little frog,' they said, 'your music is making us all unhappy.'

'I'm sorry swans, I don't want to play music that makes anyone sad.'

Next Frederick tried the harp which was rather heavy to carry. However he was soon plucking at the strings, it made such a pretty sound. He thought it sounded like raindrops falling.

His music drifted along the river and over the woods and fields. This time it bewitched the butterflies, drawn by the lovely melody. They came in their hundreds to listen to Frederick playing. There were so many butterflies, that they blotted out the sunshine. There were butterflies everywhere!

'I love the harp,' said Frederick at last, 'and I love the pretty butterflies, but there are too many.'

'How about this flute little frog?' said Otter handing him a small object that just looked like a stick with holes in it. 'It is very special and not normally for sale. Some even say it's magic.'

It was a 'magic' flute. For Frederick had only to blow on it and out came the most wonderful clear music. He knew immediately that this was the right instrument.

Very soon the riverbank and the woodlands were filled with music. The birds began to arrive. Thrushes, warblers, tits and finches. Back came the swans who were no longer sad, even the magpie who was not musical at all. Last of all came Robin and dear Blackbird. They all settled down to hear Frederick's music.

They all agreed that Frederick was a very lucky frog, for not only could he play fine music on his flute, but he was such a bright green, no one would ever want to eat him.

Frederick still shouts at times, and still gets into trouble. He really enjoys playing his flute. One thing he found out is the other creatures love him very much. It is only his *scroak* they don't like.

Why Is The Sea Salty?

Julie Merdassi

It was a hot summer's day, and Dave and his sister Sally and Mum and Dad were all going to the beach for a picnic.

'Can I take my ball?' said Dave.

'Of course you can,' said Dad, 'and don't forget your buckets and spades,' added his dad.

Sally couldn't find her swimming costume anywhere. 'Oh Mum,' she shouted, 'please come and help me look for my costume.'

'Good,' said Mum, 'now go and tell Dad to put this basket in the car, and then we'll be on our way.'

'Can I take my boat?' said Dave.

'Oh if you must,' said Mum, 'but hurry or we'll never get there.'

When they arrived at Sunnyville beach there were lots of children playing on the sand, and mums and dads were sunbathing. Sally and David hired out some deckchairs for them all to sit on.

The sea shone like sparkling gold with the sun beaming down on it. 'Can we go in the water please Mum?' asked Dave.

'Yes but be careful,' said Mum, 'we'll be watching you.'

Dave ran to the sea, carrying his blue boat, Sally took her bucket and began splashing about, kicking in the water with their tiny feet. Sally started swimming and swallowed some water, she started to cough and spat it out quickly.

'What's wrong?' said Dave.

'Urgh! Some water went in my mouth and it tasted like lots of salt.'

Dave was curious and tasted some of the water. 'I like it,' he said, and he started throwing water at Sally, making her cross.

'I'm telling Mum,' she said and went back on the sand where Mum and Dad were sitting down.

They had put up a big red umbrella to keep out the sun because it was too hot. There was lots of food on the big yellow blanket that lay on the sand. Dad gave Sally a towel. 'Here dry yourself,' he said, 'you're soaking wet.'

Dave threw lots of water all over me,' said Sally and I swallowed some and it was horrible, all salty.'

Just then Dave came over with a bucket full of seashells and pebbles.

They all started to enjoy their picnic and Sally and Dave made friends again.

After lunch Mum and Dad went for a swim and then they all went on the funfair. Sally felt quite hungry but all the food had been eaten.

'I know,' said Dad, 'we'll all have fish and chips for tea in the café.'

Sally ate her chips but complained that they had too much salt on, and they reminded her of the sea water.

Dad laughed. 'You silly girl,' he said, 'salt comes from the sea. It gets dried out and then sold in the shops for everyone to buy.'

'But why is the sea salty?' said Dave, 'and if salt is white why isn't the sea white when it's blue?'

Dad tried to explain as best he could, Sally thought she would tease Dave and told him to save his salt packet as everyone poured salt into the water who had bought fish and chips. Dave put the salt into the water. 'I can't wait to tell my teacher and friends why the sea is salty,' he said. 'I'm glad we don't put pepper in the sea, then it would be too hot.'

New Fiction Information

We hope you have enjoyed reading this book - and that you will continue to enjoy it in the coming years.

If you like reading and writing poetry drop us a line, or give us a call, and we'll send you a free information pack.

Alternatively if you would like to order further copies of this book or any of our other titles, then please give us a call or log onto our website at www.forwardpress.co.uk

New Fiction Information
Remus House
Coltsfoot Drive
Peterborough
PE2 9JX

(01733) 898101